Anyone Wanna Buy

A Heart

A Novel By Shekia Mason

This book is a work of fiction. All of the characters, organizations, and events portrayed in this novel are either products of the author's imagination or are used fictitiously.

Alicia

I smiled as I stood in the bathroom looking at myself in the mirror. My smooth, caramel skin goes perfectly with my long, golden dreadlocks. Looking at my elongated legs, it's easy to see that I'm effortlessly 5'9, which enhances the fact that I have flawlessly tight calf muscles and thighs. My breasts are a nice round C cup, perfect. As far as my backside, can you say Apple-Bottom? Heads turn when I walk in a room. I laugh out loud when I think about how even seventy-year old white men have to take a second look. I'm electric all around. I don't mean to toot my own horn but I must say that my personality is also on point.

My friends always tell me that I'm beautiful without make-up, so I rarely wear any. If you ask any one of them, they'd say that strength and independence compliment my beauty. They'd go on further, telling you how successful I am as a Real-Estate Agent. And how even though I can afford the finer things in life, I choose to be a "Plain Jane". Instead of a 7 series BMW, I drive a Honda Accord. Instead of a condo on the lake, I reside in an apartment on the north side of town. My friends would tell you that it doesn't take much to please me. But as plain as I am, everyone draws the line somewhere and I stop being simple when it comes to shoes. I have so much footwear I could open a boutique directly inside my bedroom closet. My friends have the utmost confidence in me. They only see the good.

Now ask me and you'll hear an entirely different version of the story.

I looked back into the mirror. This time I was disgusted by what I saw. My body hadn't been the same since God blessed me with that crumb snatcher of mine. I ain't even gonna lie to you; I love my son to death, but that little dude tore my body up. When I visit the mirror, there's no confidence in me. I see stretch marks and flab. All of the beauty, success, and independence left with Omar. I've tried everything to get it back since he left me. I've worked out constantly and tried every gimmick in the book to get rid of the ring of fat around my waist, but nothing has really worked. I've spent countless dollars on gym memberships, at-home work-out equipment, special diets, and every other product that's been "infomercialized".

Everything, everywhere is just right from my efforts, yet somehow the jiggle remains. And what is jiggle without stretch marks? I hate my body. I should have listened to my mother when she told me not to have kids. I can hear her now with that same old line she'd told me since I could hear her talk.

"Girl, don't have no babies. They ruin the body."

I shook my head at the thought. It was my mother's slogan. She said it often enough to make me think she'd regretted having me. That made me feel so bad, I hated to hear her say it. Therefore, I didn't listen. I tuned her out. Although, at this point in my life I wish I would have listened like my cousin Kimberlee did. Kimberlee has a husband and everything, but she still doesn't have kids. Not to mention, Kimberlee's husband is a very successful doctor. Yea, my mother's advice saved Kimberlee. But it wasn't hard for Kimberlee to hear my mother's motto: "Girl, don't have no babies. They ruin the body." My mom was only Kimberlee's aunt, so she didn't see what I saw. She didn't hear what I heard. She didn't expect what I expected. From my perspective, I couldn't admire a woman who was never there for me. My filthy rich mother made her feelings for me perfectly clear when she left me to live in a broke-down, roach infested trailer home with a grandfather that loved but couldn't afford me. I was his "Sugar Baby" and he did his best, but his best wasn't enough. "My Dear", as she made me call her because she hated the word Mama, loved men and money. She came to visit on special occasions and sent gifts in the mail, but she was never there. I've chosen to forget My Dear and anything I knew about her. She was a pain to love. A pain I could live without. Yet, somehow I just can't shake hearing her motto and being left with Paw-Paw.

"Girl, don't have no babies. They ruin the body."

I made a vow to myself at the age of sixteen to never be like her. I told myself then that I didn't want the men or the money. By

22, I decided I wanted the money, but not the men. Hmph. Up until I met Omar I could do without them. Once Omar came into my life everything changed. He was the man I didn't want to live without. There's a bruise on my heart today from when he left me. He resurrected the old Alicia; now I can't keep a man around.

There's not a man who can pleasure me: not sexually or otherwise. Something is wrong with all of them. Either they are liars, cheaters, and snakes. Or they don't have a job. Or they value the wrong things in life. Or they are gay. The sorry man list goes on and on. I've thought about doing away with them all together. You know what I mean? Take independence to a whole new level, meaning a man can't do one thing for me. However, before I could completely liberate myself again, I met Jared.

Jared has been my man for about six months. As a matter of fact, he is the reason that I'm in the bathroom now. I met him in Target over a year ago. Honestly, I wish I would have kept ignoring him but loneliness got the best of me and I finally gave in and gave him my cell phone number. I would go into the Target where he happened to work at least four days out of every week. I still don't understand my addiction to Target, I guess it's just a weakness I have. I don't feel right unless I go into that store to at least look around.

Every time I was in there, Jared would somehow walk up on me. It's not like I would happen to be on the aisle he was stocking, or something. I could be anywhere in the store, whether it was the grocery section, shoes, toys, or sporting goods, he always found me. He also always had the same excuse for trying to come up on my phone number. Each time he would compliment my dreadlocks, make small talk, then ask for the digits. It was flattering at first, then it was just flat out creepy. I'd promised myself on the way into Target that day, I would cuss him out if he merely mentioned my hair. There was no question I would see him because I always did.

I was in the greeting card section searching for the perfect card to give to my girl Tomeka for her birthday. Just as I'd expected Jared made his way to that part of the store. Sometimes, I felt like he was a walking "Alicia radar".

"What's up, Shawty?" He asked as he walked suddenly up on me.

I became immediately irritated when I turned around to find him chomping on gum like it was going out of style.

"'Sup?" I asked wryly, rolling my eyes.

He had to know I was sick of seeing him because my conversations with him had become shorter and intensely dry. It couldn't have mattered to him because he continued to chew and talk. I stood there watching his mouth move, hearing nothing but blah, blah, blah. I'd actually tuned him completely out. I was simply listening for the words *hair* or *dreads*. The moment that either of those words slipped out of his mouth, I was going to pummel him like he was doing that gum. Finally, one of the *blahs* became *dreads* and I went off. It's amazing my head didn't tumble off my neck, considering how hard I rolled it. I don't remember the exact words, but I cussed him up one side and down the other.

"Hold on Shawty. All you had to do is say no. You didn't have to cuss a brother out so bad! I'm done trying to holla at you. Peace!"

He looked genuinely upset as he turned to walk away. I didn't want to hurt Jared's feelings; I just wanted him to leave me alone. After all, he was annoying, not a bad person, so I calmed my tone.

"Sorry Jared, I'm having a bad day. What do you mean, all I had to do was say no? What was the question?

"Didn't you hear a word I said, girl? I'm tired of these braids and I wanted to know if you would start some locs for me. I've been thinking 'bout getting a haircut but I can't bring myself to do it so I figured I could try the loc thing."

I stood there thinking for a little while. Twisting my own locs was a nuisance to me so I knew I wouldn't want to maintain and re-twist Jared's hair, but I felt horrible for the tongue lashing I'd given him so I agreed to hook him up. No sooner than I agreed to start his locs, Jared was handing me his cell phone. He told me to key my number in his contact list and announced he would call me later. Then he winked at me. I should have known better than to fall for his trick. In the back of my mind I knew he was really just trying to get my number like he'd done so many times before. I was pissed that he'd gotten over on me, but I had given him my word and I wouldn't back down from it. I told Jared to call me on the following Saturday and I would "loc" him up.

Saturday swooped up on me quickly and Jared came over. By the time he arrived, I was buzzing from the Riesling I'd been sipping. I opened the door to a totally different man. Jared was sporting a slightly tilted ball cap, a pair of Black Label jeans, dark shades, and the nicest pair of Jordan's I'd seen in a while. Suddenly, he was cute to me; still not make him my man cute, but definitely make me want some TLC cute. I was sucker for a nice pair of Jordan's.

"You sure clean up well," I said with a drunk smile plastered across my face.

"Well, thanks Shawty! I try not to go everywhere in that red shirt and those khaki pants. That's a uniform. I do have other clothes, you know."

Jared laughed at me before helping himself to a seat.

By the time I finished his hair and the bottle of wine, Jared was sexy to me. He hung out for a while afterwards and helped me drink the second round of Riesling. The locs were good for him; I was glad he'd decided to get them. The way Jared licked his lips when he talked had me soaking wet. I was almost upset that he didn't make a move on me. My body was yearning for attention, so I forced him to leave before I could put my "Super Ho" cape on, and give him some ass. I asked him out for the following weekend before I sent him out the door.

Six months later, I wish Jared would have turned me down.

Don't get me wrong, he's a decent guy. He's going to make some woman real happy one day. That woman just won't be me. He's very attractive, has a job (even if it is at Target, he's trying) and he recently made a very respectable decision to go back to college to get a business degree. Jared is twenty-eight years old with no children and no attachments. He's never been married and he's not gay. Actually, Jared is almost perfect but like I told you earlier… there's always that one fault. Jared's problem is in the bedroom. He doesn't please me because he can't "swang that thang".

SHEKIA MASON

Alicia

Jared came over this morning with my favorite breakfast from Ray's Place, the mom and pop diner on my street. I wolfed down the scrambled eggs, bacon, French toast, and some butter and sugar filled grits. After breakfast I was in the kitchen putting the dishes away when he walked up on me. He did the horny man's dance, you know, the one where your man sneaks up behind you in the kitchen and moves his manhood against your butt.

"Not now, Jared." I rolled my eyes

"What's the problem? Come on baby. You know you want it, too." He kissed my neck.

The problem was he was dead wrong. I didn't want it. Why would I? He never satisfied me. Jared had the perfect package. It fit me like a lock and key, but he had no clue how to work with it. Our lovemaking was the same every time. He would climb on top of me and thrust himself in and out for less than five minutes. I would groan, more from the pain of the long hard thrusts, than from any pleasure. The more I groaned, the harder he thrust. Eventually he'd come. The end. At least it was the end for him; for me, things were just beginning. I would rush into the bathroom to get him a wet, soapy towel and toss it back out to him. Then I would turn on the shower, lock the bathroom door, and pleasure myself.

"I can't be late for work today, Jared. I have a big showing. We'll get together later." I wrestled away from his grip and rushed into the bathroom.

"Call me later baby," I yelled through the closed door.

It would be an understatement to say I was relieved to get away from Jared. Truthfully, I was trying to find a way to get rid of him on a permanent basis. He was a waste of my time because I had an itch he just couldn't scratch. That's major; I love sex.

Speaking of which, sex was the only explanation I had for being involved with the low-life brother who happened to be the real reason for these rows of skid marks across my belly. He and his sex are also why I was in that ain't going-no-where relationship for an eternity. The low-life's name is Omar and I wish I would have never met him.

Before my mind could finish the stroll down memory lane, a knock on the bathroom door snapped me away from my thoughts. It actually startled the hell out of me. It was Jared. He said he came back because he left his cell phone on my chest of drawers. Now he wanted to come into the bathroom to give me a good-bye kiss. I threw my shirt over my head and pulled my thong up before I opened the door for him. To my surprise, he was standing there with a dozen roses. He really came back to bring me flowers, said it was the anniversary of our first real date.

"We're doing it big tonight baby," Jared said, grinning like a Cheshire cat.

What could I say? I felt awful. Here I was trying to think of a way to dump Jared while he was celebrating anniversaries I didn't know existed. I decided I should put off dumping him for the moment. It didn't feel right. I rushed Jared out the door so I could finish dressing for work. Then I hurried to the bar that outlined my kitchen to set down the arrangement Jared had left for me. It was lovely, with baby's breath and airy tree ferns resting cozily between the roses. I closed my eyes, inhaled, then exhaled, basking in the jubilation of feeling loved. My jubilation left before I could blink. Reality slapped me in the face when I thought about how My Dear's love of men took her from me. I kicked the thoughts of romance and love out of my head when I remembered My Dear. Then I told them not to come back when I thought of Omar. Love is a war that I didn't want to fight. I didn't even have the time to think about it because I needed to get to work.

I grabbed my laptop bag and my cell phone, almost running to the door. Jared's pleasant, but distracting surprise had me late. My phone rang as I pulled out of my assigned parking slot.

"Hello."

"Good morning, chic!"

It was Kimberlee. She was the only person I knew who was always cheerful in the morning. Then again, she was the only one out of our clique living a dream life. She had every reason to be happy. As I've already told you she's married to a very successful doctor with his own practice so she doesn't work. She uses her entire day finding ways to spend her husband's money. There are no children to worry about and no other major responsibilities. Nothing is ever a problem for Kimberlee. I love her because she's my cousin but deep down, I'm envious. She has it all and she shows it.

"Good morning Kimberlee. What are you doing up so early? You don't have anywhere to be or anything to do.

I heard her smack her lips before she spoke.

"I have plenty to do today, starting with breakfast. Meet me at the diner on your block in fifteen minutes." She demanded.

"I can't this time. Call someone else. I have things to do." I didn't bat an eye as I rejected her invitation.

"I called you. So are you coming or not?"

"Not," I said laughing, as I tapped the end call button on my touch screen. I got a kick out of bursting Kimberlee's bubble. Hell, somebody had to do it.

She called back right away and asked me to meet her for lunch. I told her to call me around lunch time, but I didn't make any promises that I would attend. She wasn't happy about not having a full commitment but she retreated anyway. Kimberlee knew I would show up because she always got her way with me.

I zipped down Rogers Avenue with only fifteen minutes before my appointment, which happened to be a twenty-minute drive away. I would be late again. No matter how hard I tried, I was never on time.

I got my college degree in elementary education. I wanted to be a teacher until I realized I needed to be on time. My tardiness caused me to change my path and head into real estate. Becoming a Realtor was the best decision of my life. I don't have to be anywhere unless I want to. I set my own appointments and I pretty much don't have to answer to anyone. There were countless perks to real estate. Even though Karen, my broker, had a laid back personality, I needed to be on time for this appointment. She was tired of entertaining my clients because I was always running behind.

The showing went well. My buyers wanted to make an offer so we drove to my office to get started on the paperwork. Before I could finish writing the offer, Kimberlee was blowing my phone up. I sent her to voicemail three times but she was relentless. I knew she was calling to confirm our lunch plans but I wanted to finish the contract before I spoke with her. In addition to the offer, I had an Inspection and Repair Addendum to work on for a different piece of property. Despite obviously being sent to the voicemail, Kimberlee called back a fourth time.

"Hello", I purposely answered the phone in a huff, as if she were irritating me.

"Hey! Just wanted to make sure we are still on for lunch." It was apparent she didn't know she was stepping on that last nerve or she didn't care.

"I don't recall agreeing to lunch but I have to say you're definitely persistent. You just better be glad that number one I'm very hungry, and number two you're my cousin. Otherwise I would have had to cuss you out for calling me repeatedly like that. I have voicemail; leave a message."

"Anyway, name a time and place."
Once again she pretended not to hear me.

"Meet me at Winky's Seafood on the river in half an hour."

"Thirty minutes? I'm starving!" Kimberlee whined.

"Thirty minutes, or I'll take a rain check on lunch," I combated.

"Okay. You got me; see you in a little while. Bye."

"Bye."

I love Kimberlee but sometimes I have to make her understand I'm not her man. Everybody's always submitting to her and that's the problem. She is a spoiled brat and I've decided not to cater to her anymore. I wanted to show her I wasn't going to stop what I was doing just to make her happy. Yet, somehow I managed to arrive at Winky's before she did. I killed time at the bar since I always needed to have a drink to deal with Kimberlee. The bartender brought me a glass of wine to sip as I waited for my cousin to show up. I wanted to choke her for making me wait; I had other things to do.

Fifteen minutes and a second drink later, she finally sauntered into the restaurant. As usual, she looked amazing. Her wavy, coal black hair was neatly styled, and her Tom Ford jeans hugged her legs in all the right spots, accentuating her hips. She strutted over to me as if she wasn't late and stood beside the bar stool next to me. I stared her up and down before acknowledging her. Kimberlee was beautiful, which is how she always got her way. She was what men called a yellow-bone with a banging body and gorgeous features. I didn't want to tell her that she was on point but it slipped out before I could stop myself.

"You look fabulous and I hope that's why you're late," I snarled, taking a sip from my drink.

She dismissed me with a wave of her hand, then called the bartender over.

"I will have what she's having," she said, tucking her wallet underneath her arm before dismissing him with a wave and completely taking a seat.

I shook my head at her and we both laughed hysterically. Even Kimberlee realized when she was being over the top. During lunch, I could tell something was bothering her. I asked her if she wanted to talk about it but she kept denying anything was wrong. I didn't push her because I knew it would eventually come out. Instead she chose to talk about her husband, the doctor. She rambled on and on about how great everything was and she kept talking about their sex life. I hung on her every word as she described in detail how he pleased her. Something wasn't right, but I couldn't put my hand on it.

I went home after lunch because I was tired and didn't have any other appointments. Real estate allowed me to go home when I needed some 'me' time. Today was one of those days. I couldn't stop thinking about my son. He was constantly on my mind. I didn't want to do what I did. I had to. It was the only way for me to show Omar, my son's father, that I was serious. My intent had been to punish him. So far I was the only one suffering.

I walked over to my bar and poured myself another wine-glass full of Riesling. I gulped down two glasses in two swallows, without taking a breath. I rang out a long burp, wiped my mouth with the back of my hand like the wino I was becoming, then walked slowly over to the window and pulled the curtain back. I saw a young couple strolling along the walking trail that snaked its way through the park across the street from my home. Immediately, I thought of Jared, even though he wasn't the man I wanted to be walking hand in hand through the park with. If I had my choice, Omar and I would have been strolling along, holding hands. I stared out the window for a few more seconds before the tears began to roll down my face.

Omar had been the man of my dreams in the beginning. Unlike Jared, he had a package he knew how to work. He was the old adage: tall, dark, and handsome. He was thuggish, but smart. The brother wore his pants sagging, but there was nothing sagging about his intellect. He had perfect locs and the only blemish on his face was two barely noticeable tear drops lightly tattooed under his left eye. Just thinking about him had my juices flowing.

I looked out the window again. The couple in the park had disappeared and so had the bottle of Riesling. The wine took control of me fast as I made my way to the sofa to chill. I plopped down, passing out before I ever realized what hit me.

Kimberlee

I am a diva by all definitions. I love life and all it has to offer. I learned to love myself a long time ago and I learned to treat myself a long time ago. My entire life is definitely all about me. I love to shop: designer handbags, shoes, and perfumes are all of my weaknesses. I'm not talking 'bout Atlanta swap meet designer. With me, it's the real deal: Saks Fifth Avenue New York, Macy's, and small upscale boutiques. I must admit, I am spoiled by my wonderful husband, Eddie Lee Washington III. I like to call him Big Doc. You see, my husband is a doctor. He comes from a family of doctors and is very prominent in the community. Then there is Roxy and Sabri, our babies. They are just as spoiled as I am and I make sure of that. Big Doc and I have been married for the past five years but he says he knew I would be his wife from the first time we met. In the beginning, the feelings were not mutual but money has an amazing way of changing things.

My life is perfect: first and most importantly, no children. My Aunt Ola, Alicia's mom, hammered the idea of not having kids into my brain for as long as I could remember. She always told me that children ruined the body. Then I actually saw what pregnancy did to Alicia, so there's no way I'd mutilate this fabulousness in exchange for a screaming, crying, annoying mouth to feed. Oh, I bet you thought Roxy and Sabri were my children. Technically, they're not children. They are the two-year old Toy Poodles I love like my kids.

Second: no job. I wouldn't dare scar my beautiful hands filing, typing, or doing anything else that would ruin a good manicure. Don't get it twisted, I'm more than capable of working. Your girl has a master's degree in business, but I prefer the life of trophy wife. Who wants to work when you can have it all without the hassles of a job? I'm going to keep it real, being the wife of a doctor can get lonely. I miss my husband all the time because he's rarely home. We were supposed to have breakfast together this morning. It would have been the first time in more than three months. Unfortunately for me, one of his patients went into labor and he had to rush off to work.

He's always running out of the house at weird hours. If it's not when the sun meets the skyline, it's when the moon is dancing with the stars or somewhere in between. Whenever a baby decides to enter this world, Big Doc has to go. It didn't bother me in the beginning of our marriage because my husband would make sure I was satisfied before he left running. If the call came in the wee hours of the night, he would always top me off before he left. We normally didn't have a lot of time for long, hot, and steamy lovemaking but he knew how to make that five-minute quickie feel like hours of pleasure.

In spite of all the lovely things he once did for me, our relationship has slowly changed. Now instead of a steamy five minutes, I'm lucky to feel the sting from my dryness as he forces himself inside me while I'm half asleep and he's rushing out the door. I've come to the point where I hate his job. I hate his job but love the money. Well, I guess a girl can't have everything.

Rather than give up the money, I will just deal with the loneliness. It's not too bad though. I do have Tomeka, Alicia, and a host of approximately five hundred Facebook friends. When I wake up in the morning, I check my Facebook page to see what everyone is doing and to grace them all with my presence. It's kind of weird because I have virtual friends that I would never associate with in real life. I socialize with them because it's entertaining and helps me cope with the time that I spend alone. My Facebook friends don't hold a candle to my true friends, especially Alicia. She's always there for me. I know I can count on her and whether she knows it or not she can count on me. As a matter of fact, I just called her to have breakfast with me hoping she'd agree to lunch. That's the way it is between us. For some reason, Alicia is on this kick of proving to me that the world doesn't revolve around me. So if I invite her to breakfast, we meet for lunch. If I invite her to lunch, she'll agree to dinner. Go figure!

The rumbling of my stomach reminded me that I hadn't had breakfast. I called for our maid.

"Shontay!"

"What is it, Kimberlee?"

"Can you make me some eggs and bacon, please? I'm starving."

"It's already in the kitchen, sweetie." She strutted out of the bedroom.

Shontay was annoying me. I absolutely did not like to be called sweetie. It was demeaning. I called her to come back.

"Shontayyyyyyy," I sang exaggerating the latter part of her name.

"What do you want?" she chimed back.

Shontay was getting under my skin. She needed to understand that we were acquaintances, not friends, and that she was working in my home because of my mother. I wanted to fire her the same day I saw her Facebook page. All of the pictures of her with her booty shorts and half shirts were so tasteless. I didn't want her in my home flaunting her assets around my man and this bitch had the nerve to get sassy with me. All I wanted to know is how she knew I would want eggs and bacon this morning. It wasn't something I ate regularly. I didn't ask her to cook for me daily so it surprised me that she cooked breakfast before I'd asked.

However, I did tell Big Doc about my craving for scrambled eggs drenched in maple syrup. Maybe he told her.

Right now, I need to figure out why Shontay has an attitude. I don't know what's gotten into her but she's been funky acting lately. When I hired her she was so pleasant. Truth be told though, she almost didn't get the job because she was too attractive. I didn't want a beautiful woman in my home every day doing all of the domestic things I refused to do for my husband. I had no interest in ironing clothes, cooking, or washing his nasty drawers. If I had my way though, somebody's grandma would have taken that role so I wouldn't have to worry about my man and the maid. But Shontay was a family friend, and my mother had begged me to give her a job as a favor to her. Today, I regretted that decision.

I walked downstairs, trying to make it before my breakfast got cold. By the time I made it to the kitchen, Shontay was cleaning furiously. Come to think of it, she hadn't returned to the bedroom when I called her. I took my plate to the dining room, deciding I would deal with Shontay some other time.

After eating, I logged into Facebook to pass the time. I updated my status and checked out a few other pages. There was a friend request from a lady named Monica Simmons. I was sure I didn't know her but we had forty-five mutual friends so I didn't deny her request. I decided to hold off until I could determine exactly who she was. Shontay's status was a weird one, it read: "right under your nose, bitch!"; something typical for the likes of her.

A few hours later, I was hungry again and still lonely so I called Alicia until she answered. Once I talked to her to confirm our lunch plans, I went into my walk-in closet and got top-notch before heading out to meet her.

The pan-seared Atlantic salmon, wine, and time with Alicia was exactly what I needed before I went back home. I wanted to stop by the mall but wasn't in much of a shopping mood. My relationship with Big Doc was taking its toll and I felt myself getting depressed. I knew Alicia was bored out of her mind, hearing me ramble on and on about my loving husband. Little did she know it was all to mask the pain. Things were not the same but I didn't want anybody to know.

I spent the drive home reminiscing about the good ole days when Big Doc and I began dating. I laughed for a brief second as I thought about the big, less than stylish, horn-rimmed glasses that he wore in college. Big Doc wasn't initially the best catch. When I met him, he didn't even have potential. He was tall and lanky with that Michael Jackson syndrome: high water pants. Even with pearly-white, braces-straightened teeth, his smile was still awkward. Eddie Lee was a virgin then. Hell, he'd never even been looked at by a woman, until he had me on his arm. Once he'd bought my love, I cleaned him up and made him who he is today. Who does he think he is now? Success has gone to his head, and he is killing me. I yelled for Shontay as soon as I opened the door. I needed more wine and I wanted Shontay to grab it for me.

My mind was consumed with thoughts about the time in my life when my husband was available. It didn't help at all when Alicia started to ramble on and on about six dollar an hour Jared. Although she tried hard, she wasn't fooling anyone but herself pretending like she'd found a great guy. I knew his type. Jared was a punk who was trying to get whatever he could from a woman. What could he do for her working at Target? Alicia needs to get like me. She needs a man with money, esteem, and class. I keep trying to tell her that I wouldn't settle for less but she believes I'm just hating. Me, hate? I would never do that. I'm simply trying to help her out. All the horrible thoughts about Jared had me thinking about my marriage. No matter how much I dogged Alicia out, my mind drifted back to my house. Big Doc and I hadn't spent any time together in a few months. I sat down solemnly on my bed. How long would I be able to keep up the facade? My husband hadn't touched me in more than three weeks; not even once for a quickie.

There had been a time in my life when Big Doc couldn't keep his hands off me. Once upon a time we were getting busy two or three times a day, but those days were long gone, and now I've resorted to almost begging him for sex, something I would never admit to my friends. The stories I shared with them during our sex-filled talks at Mary Love's were things I read in Zane novels. I'm surprised that no one has ever called me out on that.

My stomach started to tighten up and the wetness of tears formed in my eyes. Where was Shontay? I needed my wine!

"Shontay," I screamed angrily.

"What-do-you-want?" She chopped her words as if I were annoying her.

I wanted to slap her.

"Shontay," I spoke slowly. "I would like a bottle of wine from the rack in the kitchen, that's only if it's not too much trouble." I continued to speak slowly, exhaling at the end. Shontay was trying my patience again.

She didn't speak at all as she sauntered out of the room. I swear as soon as I have a chance, I'm going to start interviewing for her position because Shontay must go. Meanwhile, I have to devise a plan to regain my husband's interest. I love this man, my college sweetheart, to death but if he doesn't give me some release soon, I might have to go postal on him. And what he better realize is that I'm crazy enough to do just that!

Tomeka

Malik's been hard on my feelings for at least six months. How can he stay mad so long, over something as minimal as a woman getting her groove on? I've wrestled with it for a while and have come to the conclusion that Malik is being absolutely ridiculous. I remember distinctly what made him mad.

It was my 30th birthday celebration. Instead of doing it big like we could have, Malik and I decided to throw a small, private house party. Only our closest friends and some family were invited. Everyone was mingling and we were all having a good time. However, a good time wasn't what I wanted. I wanted to have a great time. After all, you only turn thirty once in a lifetime. Thirty was a big number for me; it took me further into the depths of adulthood and I was ready. I remember having to pull Alicia out of the house when she hit the big 3-0. She cried all day at the thought of growing old but for me, turning thirty meant I was still alive and called for celebration.

I cranked the music up and started to dance. A crowd formed around me as I rocked and swayed my hips. Everyone clapped and cheered me on.

"Go Meka! Go Meka!"

With alcohol in my system and encouragement from the crowd, I dipped to the floor.

"Go Meka! Go Meka!"

I dipped again. In my mind, I was rocking the crowd. Before I knew what happened, everyone joined me. We all rocked, swayed, and dipped together. I quickly scanned the room looking for Malik. I wanted to dance with my man. When my eyes finally found him, I stopped dancing mid-dip. He was standing on the wall, left hand in his pocket, angrily watching my every move as his right hand stroked his chin. Malik was mad.

I walked over to him.

What's wrong with you?" I asked concerned, but irritated at the same time.

"Nothing."

I hate when Malik lies to me. He was obviously bothered by something but I wasn't in the mood for entertaining his mess so I ignored the lie.

"Dance with me," I said, rubbing his free hand.

He shook his head, "I don't want to dance."

His answer was final. I walked away without trying to convince him otherwise. It was my birthday for Pete's sake and I didn't plan to spend my day begging Malik to be happy. If he wanted to be a sourpuss, that was his right.

I made my way around the room to thank everyone for coming. When I approached Eddie Lee, he wasn't his usual fun-loving self. He seemed quieter than normal. Come to think of it, his Siamese twin, sidekick of a wife, wasn't dangling from his arms. Maybe they were going through something. It wasn't my business. I pretended not to notice his demeanor, cordially thanked him for coming to my party, then turned to walk away. He grabbed my shirttail, pulling me back to him.

"Happy birthday," He said, hugging me.

The hug was very soft and friendly. Eddie Lee didn't say anything other than happy birthday, but the hug felt weird, almost flirtatious.

"Thank you," I stammered, taken aback. "Thank you," I repeated, backing away from him.

I wanted to run like Forest Gump, away from my thoughts about Eddie Lee. That hug was eerily wrong, but I liked it. I wanted him to hug me longer and harder.

My actions contradicted my thoughts as I managed to move away from Kimberlee's husband. Being in his presence was an accident waiting to happen. I looked back at him one last time as I walked away. The look in his eyes scared me; it was out of place. It told me he wanted me.

By the time I finished working the room and back to Malik, he was even more frustrated.

"You need to sit down and stop being slutty."

I closed my eyes for a moment while I determined my response.

"Slutty, Malik? Seriously? Just what did I do that was slutty?"

"You are thirty years old today. You should be ashamed about the way you paraded around on the dance floor. Act your age, Meka."

Malik's eyes tightened and his jaw twitched when he spoke to me. They were perfect indicators of his frustration.

"Please tell me this is a joke Malik. Are you saying you don't want ME to dance at MY party? This has got to be a joke."

I laughed.

"You're the only one laughing."

Malik's eyes dared me to laugh again.

I didn't take his dare. I simply turned and walked away.

I couldn't believe Malik had the nerve to be mad because I danced. I'm glad he didn't see Eddie Lee hug me. I'm sure he would've blown a gasket. It was sexy. A chill ran down my back to my thighs. The thought of it sent more pulsating chills all over my body. Shame forced me to hold my head down. I told myself it was harmless. Over and over, I reminded myself that Eddie Lee was Kimberlee's husband. I looked up in time to confirm my thoughts. Eddie Lee and Kimberlee were leaving the dance floor, arm in arm. Her face glowed as if she were in Heaven in his arms. I wondered how it felt to be loved by a real man. Eddie Lee was a great catch. Malik paled in comparison.

I spent the rest of the night disappointed by Kimberlee's bliss. It's a sad shame how I allowed myself to feel that way, but I did.

The dance floor called me out to groove all my displeasure away; instead I stood with my back to the wall to avoid Malik's wrath.

I should have packed my bags and left him the night of my birthday party. I didn't do it, though. Although I was doing bad with Malik, I would've been worse without him. This old heart of mine… I'd rather have it bruised than broken any day.

Yeah. We're still together.

Alicia

I rolled out of bed around eleven o' clock that night. I'd been napping since three in the afternoon so my body yearned for a relaxing bath. I dragged myself into the bathroom at a snail's swiftness and leaned over the tub to turn on the water and adjust it to the perfect temperature. I liked to fill the tub halfway full with steaming water that I could barely sit in and allow cold water to trickle from the faucet while I drank wine and listened to Pandora Radio. The trickle of the water created the ideal atmosphere and cooled my bath down at the right pace. I sank down into the tub under the bubbles, closed my eyes, and washed the sleep away from me. Before I could stop them, my thoughts went to Omar and his slim, muscular body. Just remembering our nights of passion had me tingling all over.

I couldn't stop myself from going back to the night of my first date with Omar. After we went bowling, Omar stopped by the liquor store before heading toward my apartment.

"What do you drink?" He asked me as he let the kickstand down on the sleek, black BMW K 1200 motorcycle I was sitting on the back of.

"Budweiser," I answered.

"Budweiser is a man's drink. Stay put. I know just the thing for you," he said with authority as he undid the chin strap on his helmet.

Omar was in and out of the beer store with quickness. I was a few steps ahead of him as we walked down the cracked sidewalk toward my building. I knew he was looking at my butt so I put a little extra twist in my walk. I stopped abruptly as I reached the door. He bumped into me and lingered just a bit before backing away.

"Sorry," he mumbled.

I pushed the key in the lock without responding. Once inside my apartment, I became the authority, speaking to him as he had done me earlier.

"Sit down," I said, pointing to the love seat, which was just in front of the door. I didn't break stride as I headed to my bedroom to remove my shoes.

When I entered the hallway, headed back into the living room, he was standing there with two wine glasses. I stopped and stared at him, biting my bottom lip. We stared at each other for a moment. I was very relaxed as we continued to stare. I could feel the cream oozing out of me.

Not on the first date, I thought to myself.

I knew I had to get it together. He almost had me out of my panties without speaking a word. I gathered myself and looked at him with a stone face.

"What the hell are you doing? I thought I asked you to have a seat," I hissed.

"My bad li'l mama," he said, walking toward me.

I put my hand in his face. "And don't ever call me li'l mama, I hate that shit!"

"Damn, girl. I'm sorry. Why are you being so rude, do you want me to leave or something?

"No, don't leave but I do want you to mind your manners while you are in my home."

"I can dig it," he said walking back to the sofa he was supposed to be sitting on.

"I bought you a nice Riesling wine. You need to get off the Budweiser's. You're a lady."

I wrinkled my nose at him. If I'd wanted wine, I would have asked for wine. I wanted a beer but I decided I wouldn't be hard on him. I would drink his wine and buy some beer the next day. I took the glass from his hand and sipped. The Riesling was sweet, not overbearing. It had a nice feel going down and best of all, it gave me a buzz.

I listened intently as Omar talked to me about his dreams. He had long-term goals. He wanted to get his college degree so he could coach inner city youth who lived the same type lifestyle he did as a kid. He wanted to promote Hip-Hop concerts in the summer when he wasn't coaching. He had a dream of living comfortably financially and one day raising a family. Sure, he wasn't quite there. He was hustling street pharmaceuticals and he had a son he wasn't allowed to see, but one day he would not have to grind because his bank account would be stacked and he would settle down with a wife and a child he could raise. I think I fell in love that night, right after he laid out his dreams.

I didn't intend to love Omar. In fact, I had absolutely no intentions of even seriously dating him or anybody else for that matter. I'd convinced myself years before that I could live without a man. I learned to depend only on me to get by. If something in my apartment was broke, I could fix it. I was my own "Mrs. Fix-It". I had my own money and could take care of myself in every way. My grandfather taught his "Sugar Baby" about cars so I didn't need a man's help with my ride either.

I smiled as I thought about the good ole days with Paw-Paw. We'd hang out under the shade tree, heads beneath the hood of Betsy, Paw-Paw's old Ford that he was always working on but never quite fixed. I learned to change the oil, the tires, check the battery cables, and all of my fluids under that same tree. Thank God for my Paw-Paw. Because of him, I didn't need a man. I was doing just fine; then Omar came. It was almost as if he forced me to love him. I'd even told Omar that I didn't want to love him. He'd laugh and say "You won't be able to help yourself!". He was so sexily cocky.

Everything after the first date happened at the speed of light. Before I knew it, many nights of pillow talk had me deep in love with Omar, just as he'd predicted. He told me he loved me numerous times before I opened my heart to him.

Without instruction from me, my face constructed a scowl, which nudged me back to reality. It pissed me off to think about how Omar totally disregarded my heart. I told him that I'd lost everyone I ever loved and he promised he'd never leave me. But he did it anyway; he disappeared on me like a thief in the night.

A knock on my front door jarred me all the way back to the present. I glanced at the wall clock to get the time. It was after midnight. Who could be knocking at this hour?

Jared hugged me before he could get in the door.

I instinctively pushed him off, "What the hell have I told you about coming over without calling, especially at this hour?"

He lowered his head, pushing his lips onto mine. He kissed me before he spoke a word.

"I've been calling since four o'clock this evening. I thought something was wrong so I drove over to check on you."

"I'm fine, Jared. Thanks," I said dryly, not moving away from the door. I wasn't in the mood for him, not while Omar was on my mind.

The look on his face told me that I'd hurt his feelings by being curt but that did not detour him. He stood directly in front of me for a second without saying anything.

When he finally spoke, he asked me if I planned to let him in. I moved to the side of the door, still holding onto the knob, and let him pass. I gently closed the door before disappearing down the hallway into my bedroom. Jared quickly followed me, unaware he had struck a nerve by popping up. I made my way into the bathroom to finish soaking but Jared stopped me before I disrobed.

"You smell good, baby. You know I love your cucumber melon scented body wash." Jared had trailed me into the bathroom.

I tried to speak but he covered my mouth with his index finger. He pecked up and down my neck and face, looking intently into my eyes whenever he wasn't kissing. He kissed more and more, grabbing my backside and pulling me closer to him. He gently tugged the belt, which was looped through my silk robe, until my robe opened, revealing my nakedness. He licked his full, juicy lips before leaning in to kiss me on the mouth. He looked so… so… stupid! He was not turning me on at all, especially when I thought about how he was the only one who benefitted from our sexual escapades. Insults overflowed in my mind; I wanted to open the flood gates, unleashing a myriad of insults, but I refrained.

"Jared, sweetie, I'm not in the mood," I said hesitantly. "I've just had the worst day of my life. All I wanna do is go to bed," I lied, pretending to whine.

He pulled his head back and pushed himself away from me. He retreated to the bed, disappointed.

"I came over because I thought something was wrong. We were supposed to be celebrating our anniversary tonight, but you haven't answered the phone at all today," he said, sounding defeated.

Jared was right. I had completely slept the day away, even though we were supposed to be spending time together. My mind told me to finish him off by asking him to leave. My heart told me to make him feel better. I listened to my heart. I allowed my robe to fall to the floor as I walked seductively over to the bed. With one finger, I pushed him. He fell back, staring up at me, with his jaw dropped in utter amazement. Jared had never seen me completely nude, although he'd practically begged for us to make love openly without the restraints of darkness. My apprehensions about the stretch marks that decorated my abdomen had always prevented it. However, tonight was our anniversary and I owed Jared an apology. There was no question about Jared's feelings for me. He kissed every inch of my body, paying special attention to the imperfections on my skin that looked like tiger stripes. He licked and kissed each line one by one, making me feel beautiful all over.

"Words cannot express how you make me feel, Alicia. I think I'm falling in love with you... every inch of you."

I didn't respond with words because I didn't know what to say. I didn't love Jared but I didn't want to hurt his feelings so I simply kissed him on the forehead before rolling over to go to sleep.

The next morning was like a breath of fresh air because Jared had already left for work by the time I woke up. A note on the pillow replaced his body:

Good morning baby. Last night was wonderful. I would love for you to stand me up more often. (SMILE) ☺. I made you pancakes for breakfast. They are in the microwave. See you tonight.

I read the note through narrowed eyes, allowing a faint smile to sweep across my face. Jared's words warmed my heart, making me want to open it up to him. I cringed at the thought of loving someone again. To me, love was as poison and inevitable as death. I'd worked hard not to care for anybody since Omar, My Dear, and Paw-Paw. They were the only people besides my son that I ever truly loved, and all of them were taken from me suddenly and without cause. My Dear and Omar took immediate and voluntary exits out of my life. But my Paw-Paw died when I was barely nineteen.

For Paw-Paw, it was peaceful. He died in his sleep like he'd always prayed for, at the ripe old age of ninety-five. He was ready to go. I'm sure of it because he told me daily, "You know Sugar-Baby, Paw-Paw won't always be here to look after you. I'm getting old and tired child. You have to get yourself together because your mama ain't worth a penny with a hole in it, so you'll be alone when I go home to be with Jesus." I cried every time he said it because the truth hurt more than bullets and my Paw-Paw meant everything to me.

I knew something was wrong when I went by that Sunday morning to check on him. My Paw-Paw was up before the rooster crowed every day of the week. By 4 am, he was awake with his radio tuned to the news, sitting in the back door of his old trailer, smoking rolled cigarettes and drinking whiskey. He'd sit in the same spot all day, unless he was working on Betsy. I'd come by each Sunday to bring him dinner from Mrs. Bennie, one of the nice big hat church ladies. Mrs. Bennie was sweet on Paw-Paw, but she already had an old ball and chain to contend with and didn't need another one. I opened the front door with Paw-Paw's spare key; it was eerily quiet in the house. I could hear blues on the radio playing faintly in the background, which immediately scared me because Paw-Paw only listened to the blues when he was laying down for bed. It was well after noon. Paw-Paw should have been up by now. I'm not sure why, but I tip-toed farther inside the house.

"Paaaaaaw-Paaaaaaw," I sang.

I waited for him to call back to me.

My heart pounded in my chest. "Paaaaw-Paaaaw," I said again, only louder this time.

When my Paw-Paw didn't answer, I knew instantly that my biggest fear had come to pass. The walk down the hall to his bedroom was torture. I peeked my head around the corner before going in. My eyes bugged wide, then snapped closed. I'm still haunted by the image of my Paw-Paw lying in his bed, one hand over his heart, the other serenely at his side. I moved closer to him.

"Paw-Paw?" This time it was a question. I hoped for an answer, even though it was apparent Paw-Paw had met his maker. I would've done anything to hear his raspy voice reply back, "Paw-Paw's fine, Sugar Baby."

Creepy silence answered instead. Again, I moved slowly closer. I stood over the bed, looking down at the love of my life. I stared for five minutes. He wasn't breathing. My hands moved on their own to massage his silky-smooth, black skin. I raked his scruffy, snow-white beard with my fingers, as my tears landed on his cheek. Then I rubbed the top of his head, where hair should have been, but a receding hairline had stolen most of it early on.

Paw-Paw was gone.

My head went to his chest; my arms around his neck.

"Nooooo Paw-Paw! Nooo! Please don't leave me. You're all I got!"

I tried to hug my Paw-Paw back to life as I sobbed uncontrollably. Once I pulled myself together, I hugged him again for the last time. I was amazed by the fact that I didn't run fast from the room. I hated the thought of death. I didn't want to talk about it or see anyone lifeless like Paw-Paw was. Death scared me; its smell disturbed me. Somehow, Paw-Paw didn't have the smell of death all over him, though. His clothes reeked simply of rolled cigarettes and whiskey.

I gave him a final kiss goodbye, then I called the ambulance to come take my Paw-Paw away. I sat on the porch and waited for them to come. Our ongoing chess game was still on the table. Paw-Paw could have ended it months ago, but he loved to play the game so he prolonged it. In retrospect though, he may have kept it going to keep me coming back. He should have known that I would always come back anyway. Head in my hands, I cried a river right on the porch. I'd never see Paw-Paw or My Dear again. Paw-Paw was right about her; she didn't love anybody but herself and she proved it when she didn't come back for the funeral.

I hurried to the bathroom to wash my tear-stained face. Love drained me. I took a deep breath, then a quick look in the mirror to regain my composure. Crying over Paw-Paw and My Dear couldn't increase my funds, so I had to get to work.

Tomeka

I sat straight up in bed, and my eyes popped open all in one motion.

"Did you hear that, Malik?" I asked my boyfriend as I jumped out of bed.

"Yesssss…" he answered in his sleep.

"What was it?" I whispered.

Malik didn't budge but I didn't have time to waste trying to wake him. He hadn't slept in three days so I knew it would be useless to keep bugging him unless there was a true emergency. I briefly thanked God that I was a hustler's girl as I slid my hand under Malik's pillow, reaching for his nine millimeter pistol. We'd had countless arguments about that gun being in the house, but tonight it came in handy. It sounded like gunfire outside, and although I wasn't certain I wouldn't have stepped a foot out of my bedroom if I didn't have protection. Before I made it out of out to investigate, there was a loud banging on our front door. The two pit bulls in our back yard barked furiously. Something was wrong. I pulled the safety down on the gun and cocked it. With my finger on the trigger of that steel peacemaker, I screamed through the door, "Who is it?"

There was no answer. I was getting antsy; my trigger finger shook nervously. I was about to plaster the front door with bullet holes.

The person on the outside screamed, "It's your neighbor and someone has been shot in your driveway!"
I didn't open the door. I ran back to the bedroom to wake Malik. This was his mess; he needed to deal with it.

"Get up, somebody's been shot in our driveway!" I screamed, viciously shaking him.

He jumped up, slid into his basketball shorts and headed for the front door. I handed him the gun as he ran past me.

"Nine-one-one, what's your emergency?"

"I need an ambulance and the police. There's been a shooting!"

The operator on the other end of the phone repeated my statements as if she didn't hear me. She followed up with a series of, in my opinion, unnecessary questions. I gave her the address and advised her that I didn't have any further information. She kept pressing me so I demanded that she send the police and ambulance then I disconnected the call. I didn't have time for nonsense; I had bigger fish to fry. Someone had been shot in my driveway, the police were on the way, and our garage was filled with mounds of weed that Malik had promised me would be gone by morning. I definitely didn't need this. I ran to the twins' bedroom to cry. It's sad to say, but I really didn't care who'd been hurt outside. I saw the blue and red flashing lights through the bedroom window. I refused to go out there. All I wanted to do was sit on the floor and cry.

I told Malik it was time to get out. I told him daily, yet he insisted on doing what he did. He told me everything was part of being the girl of a hustler. He was right. This lifestyle had its perks. We were never broke. I was the only one of our friends who could keep up with Kimberlee and her lavish shopping sprees. I was with her every time she hit the Gucci store.

The money wasn't the only thing but it was certainly the main thing. All of the other perks like jewelry, clothes, shoes, and the freedom to travel were all benefits of the money. My honey made sure our home was laid and that I drove one of the finest cars money could buy. What did I have to complain about? Malik took us from the hood. We're a family. I should be happy. But I'm not. Money can't take away the fear that Malik will leave us. It can't take away the nightmares I have in the middle of the night or the night sweats, and it damn sure can't take away the fact that someone had been shot in my driveway.

I opened the curtains. The street was swarmed with policemen, firemen, and paramedics. I prayed to God, asking him to spare the life of the victim. I asked him to make this a wake-up call for Malik, and I prayed the shooter hadn't been coming for my family. I told God if the victim lived, I would change my life forever.

Malik was big in the game. He'd been dealing drugs since I met him in junior high. The sad thing is he really didn't have to hustle. His family was well off. Both his parents had survived the hood and made something of themselves. His dad's furniture business had afforded them a wealthy lifestyle. They lived in the hood because they wanted to, not because they had to.

Malik was a straight A student and star athlete. He'd been given an opportunity to go to college on a full basketball scholarship. During our high school days, I was sure Malik would follow the right path. He had his head on straight until he let peer pressure get the best of him. We'd talked about it plenty of times. I always asked him why he chose the streets. I wondered why he didn't give basketball a fair chance. Malik was good enough to play professionally, but he was addicted to hustling. During every conversation, Malik reminded me he was no punk. It never made sense to me. It had to be a man thing. I knew from our talks he'd succumbed to peer pressure early on, and it shaped the rest of his life. Instead of going to basketball practice, he chose to hang out with the same hooligans who called him punk. He didn't want to look soft to them so he chose the streets. Something about fast money and pride made sense to him. I understood his rationale to a certain extent but Malik needed to realize he was a man now. It was time to do man things.

My thoughts were interrupted by the phone. It was a friend of mine who lived at the end of our cul-de-sac. She was being nosey, so I let the phone ring.

My view of the window allowed me to see that the ambulance and fire trucks were gone but the police still lingered. This couldn't be happening. I lit a cigarette to calm my nerves. I didn't know who'd been shot, or what the police were talking to Malik about. All I knew was I had asked Malik not to bring those drugs into our home and I was going to blast him as soon as this was over.

Thirty minutes passed before Malik came back. He was visibly shaken but relieved. The guy who'd been shot was a friend of the neighbor across the street. He'd been followed from a party by the jealous boyfriend of a girl he'd danced with. On the way to his friend's house, he'd mistakenly pulled in our yard and was shot before he could make it to the front door. The man who'd followed him fired four shots from his car, hitting his rival once in the stomach. It seemed as if the victim would survive. The police were off to catch the shooter so they had no reason to come into our home. It was a blessing, and I was going to change my life. The problem would be getting Malik to make the same sort of changes.

Malik removed his basketball shorts and T-shirt, then climbed back into bed as if nothing happened.

"Turn off the lights and let's get some sleep. It's already three-thirty and we have to be up by six." He yawned.

My nose turned up instantly without any help from me. *"We?"* I thought. I had to get up at six o'clock to get the twins ready. Malik lay in bed and watched me so he could tell me to turn the lights out as soon as I finished. I stood there watching him drift off to sleep as if nothing had happened. It confused me to think he wasn't bothered by the whole ordeal. I needed to smoke.

"I'm not sleepy, Malik."

"What do you mean you're not sleepy? It's three-thirty... no excuse me, it's three-thirty-one in the morning. You better lay down, woman."

Malik chuckled a little, but I knew he was serious as a heart attack.

"Malik."

Silence.

"Malik."

"What baby? Damn, I'm sleepy."

"I just wanna talk to you," I said behind a sigh.

"What the hell can we talk about right now, that can't wait? Huh, Meka? And sho' don't tell me that you wanna talk about the incident that just happened. It didn't have nothing to do with us. You heard what I said. Now turn off the light, turn on the fan, and lay down."

I didn't say anything back to him. I didn't feel like arguing. It was always whatever Malik said. Not Simon says. Malik says. I did as I was told then grabbed my pack of cigarettes. I wanted to go outside to get some fresh air, but there was no way that I was going out there. Someone had been shot in my driveway, and it was going to take a while for me to forget that.

I rubbed my face with both hands. That was to keep the tears from flowing freely down my cheeks, but it didn't help. I wanted to sit down in the living room and smoke the whole pack of cigarettes. My nerves needed to be calmed. I was still shaking. I walked to my kids' room to check on them. They were sound asleep, without a care in the world. I loved them so much. They deserved better than this.

Any of us could have been shot tonight. I turned out of their bedroom and went to the kitchen, figuring I might as well snack since I was awake. The refrigerator was stocked full, but I didn't see anything I wanted to eat so I grabbed a beer instead. I sat in the dark without the television on and sipped my beer.

Along with the beer, I smoked two cigarettes before I noticed I wasn't getting a buzz, so I reached behind the wrappings of my cigarettes package for my emergency stash: a small bud of weed and one joint paper. I didn't smoke often but tonight was one of the times that warranted a good high. I rolled, licked, tucked, then puffed. The first puff gave me a tingle so I smoked until it was gone. I can't say I didn't feel the effects of the marijuana. The room was thick; my mind was racing.

I promised God I would change. I was raised a minister's daughter. I know better. What am I doing here with Malik? Why do I let him control everything? My kids and I could have been hurt tonight, or even worse, I could have shot somebody because Malik didn't hear the gunshots or move. I shouldn't be smoking weed, or drinking. Hell, I shouldn't be shacked up with Malik. It's not worth losing my soul. I have to straighten up. I'm leaving Malik. I hate him... but only because I love him so much. It's true what they say: it's a thin line between love and hate. If only Malik would change his life with me. We could make it official, get married, and be a family. I know he won't change, though. Actually, I probably won't change. I've had this conversation with myself a million times. I never do the right thing, but I need to do the right thing. Tomorrow is not promised. Tomorrow is not promised. Man! I shouldn't have smoked that reefer, I'm tripping now.

I wasn't sleepy but the effects of the marijuana had me paranoid so it was time for me to lie down. I tip-toed in the room and softly eased under the covers with Malik. I tried to stay on my side of the bed without touching him. As soon as my head hit the pillow, Malik looked at me with one eye open.

"Are you okay, baby?"

"Yep, I'm fine," I whispered.

I scooted closer to him. He wrapped his arms securely around me.

"I love you, Meka. You and my sons mean the world to me." He kissed me on the forehead and closed his eyes.

"I love you too," I said, trying to get comfortable in his arms. "Good night, Malik."

"Good night, baby," he said, then snored.

I wasn't as content as my boyfriend, so I lay there in the dark for a while without moving because I didn't want to wake him. I knew he was beat. Seconds became minutes, minutes hours. I'm not sure how long I lay there before I fell asleep but I heard another noise. It kind of sounded like someone had opened my bedroom door, but Malik's arm was still around me so I knew it wasn't him. Maybe it was one of the boys. Just as I opened my eyes to check on them, a hand was coming down over my face. I tried to scream but no sound escaped my lips. My eyes could not lie. There was a man dressed in all black in my bedroom with his hand over my mouth.

I sat up in the bed frantically searching the room. No one was here but me and Malik. He was sleeping like a baby. I did a walk-through of our home with Malik's gun. No one was there. I'd been dreaming.

Alicia

It was a little after noon when I arrived at the office. My son's picture was sitting on the edge of my desk. His eyes followed me across the room chastising me. I tried my best to ignore the feelings that were building in the pit of my stomach as I leaned behind the desk chair to plug in my laptop. Little Omar was handsome. The older he got, the more he resembled his father. They shared the same silky, dark skin, and beautiful brown eyes. As a matter of fact, I couldn't pinpoint whether Little Omar looked more like his dad or my grandpa. Hindsight being 20/20, the three of them bore a striking resemblance, which could possibly explain the extreme love I have for Omar. Could it be that he reminded me of Paw-Paw?

What a day this was turning into. I didn't want to cry anymore, but I couldn't fight it. I grabbed the frame and kissed the picture. A single tear barreled its way down my face onto the frame.

"Alicia." The secretary was calling me over the intercom.

"Yes, Belinda?"

"You have a client waiting," she almost sang.

I walked to the front, where a brown-skinned lady I immediately recognized stood waiting.

"Hello, Mrs. Young," I greeted her.

She shook my hand, then followed me into my office. I gestured for her to take a seat. Mrs. Young was a sophisticated-looking, very attractive, heavy set woman. She was also very wealthy and had come into her money by keeping a sugar daddy. Not just any man would do. The men she was with had to be able to afford her. Mrs. Young spent a great deal of money with me. Her latest sucker was a real estate tycoon who had no idea she was making real estate investments with me. I'm sure she would have loved to give him the business, but the problem was she didn't want him to know she was using his money to do it. Poor Mr. Tycoon- he thought his generous donations were being spent to fund lavish shopping sprees and trips to beautiful islands. However, Sandra Young was no fool at all. She was preparing for a great retirement. She would take the money he'd given her and go on a three weekend hiatus in town when he thought she was on a cruise and not spend the money until she'd saved enough to invest in a property. Unlike her sugar daddy, who was dealing in million-dollar properties, she was making a lot of small investments hoping for the "big payoff".

I was pleasantly surprised to see her because she hadn't called to make an appointment. Come to find out, this wasn't a business call. Mrs. Young wanted to talk to me about something personal.

After our conversation, I needed a break so I left the office and walked three doors down to the nail salon. Obviously, every woman in the city wanted a manicure and pedicure because the place was jam packed.

"May I help you?" the Asian nail stylist asked in broken English.

"I need a fill-in," I answered, waving my fingers in front of my face.

"You wait li'l bit," she stated, continuing to butcher her words.

I sat down in the waiting area and grabbed an *Essence* magazine. Beyonce' graced the cover looking like she'd just stepped off the runway. I looked around the room trying to figure out exactly how long of a wait a li'l bit was. Sitting to the right of me was a young, white lady with a small child attached to her wrist by way of a leash. I frowned at her. The leash annoyed me. For the life of me I didn't understand what would possess a woman to "leash" her child. Surely, not love. Watching her pull her wandering toddler back to her by a monkey's tail was as painful as crawling through a tunnel of iron thorns. I simply didn't understand. But then again, how could I understand? I am the same woman who's brought to tears by the sight of her child's picture. The same little girl who has never been allowed to address her mother as such. My Dear was strict when it came to how I addressed her. I remembered a time when she back hand slapped me for calling her Mama in the grocery store. Of course, I'd never understand the psychology of a love so deep that it caused a mother to obsess enough to "leash" her child.

My overworked tear well filled for the billionth time. The feeling in the pit of my stomach was all too familiar. I could feel my throat tighten. My voice was waiting to crack. My brief flashback to Kimberlee's perfect Aunt Ola, my mother, had me frozen in the chair. I took a couple deep breaths to ward off the overflow of emotions that attempted to smother me. With my tears suppressed, I stood from my seat. I didn't wait to have my nails filled. I needed to get home to the last of my Riesling so I excused myself from my seat and walked to my car.

The drive home was cleansing. My suppressed tears were released and sped past my chin in a race with my thoughts. Every time I re-lived My Dear, Paw-Paw came with her. It was like they were a pair. My Dear should have loved me. My Paw-Paw did love me. He's the only man who ever did. I miss him so much. There's a hole in my heart where he used to be. Paw-Paw's presence is irreplaceable. He was my grandfather, my brother, my uncle, and my daddy all rolled into one. He played every male role in my life. My biological dad is a stranger to me. I've never been introduced to any man as his daughter. Knowing My Dear, though, my dad is probably somewhere close, and I've probably seen him infinite times. It's strange, because I've always dreamed of meeting him. In my dreams, my daddy was a great man like

Martin Luther King, Jr. I was convinced he didn't know I existed because a great man would never live in this cruel world without regard to his daughter. In my dreams, my dad loved me more than Paw-Paw did. He took me to the park and pushed me on the swings. He bought me dolls, nail polish, and clothes. He kissed me on my forehead and called me Sugar Baby. No, he called me Princess because only Paw-Paw called me Sugar Baby. My dad was perfect in my dreams, but in reality, I didn't even know his name.

Aside from Paw-Paw, Marcus was the only other man who could have possibly loved me. When I was a little girl, I believed he loved me. Marcus was the only boyfriend I'd known My Dear to have. He was always nice to me when she was around, but he showed me he loved me when she wasn't. At least that's what he told me. Every time My Dear went some place that she couldn't take me Marcus would babysit me. He told me daily how much he loved me. When she was gone he'd kiss me on the lips and rub me where my boobs would have been if I was a grown woman. His favorite way to show love was to bounce me on his lap while I was naked. I always cried because it hurt like hell, but I didn't complain because Marcus told me that love was supposed to hurt. I knew he was telling the truth because I'd heard My Dear tell her best friend, Carolyn the same thing many times with tears in her eyes. My Dear cried countless nights because of something

Marcus did. But she never cried harder than the night that I told her about Marcus's snake.

I was in first grade before I realized I'd been molested. A police officer came to our classroom to talk to us about bad people; strangers that kidnapped kids, and even familiar people who hurt kids. He talked to us about people like Marcus, then advised all of us to tell someone that we could trust if we were ever hurt by another adult. I trusted My Dear. She had never hurt me before that night. So when I got home, I told her that Marcus showed me a snake in his pants. Then I told her how Marcus told me the snake loved me and he made me touch it. He even asked me to kiss it. Marcus got really mad at me when I told him I didn't like snakes. My Dear fell to her knees. She was overcome with anger and sent me to my room until Marcus came home. My Dear took me and Marcus into the woods, down a long, dark dirt road. She and Marcus got out of the car, leaving me alone. I was terrified and cried until My Dear returned without Marcus. Immediately afterwards, My Dear hauled me down to the country and dropped me off to Paw-Paw. After that, I saw My Dear sporadically throughout my life on special occasions, until eventually she disappeared completely. She'd left me with Paw-Paw because I told her about Marcus. I wish I could take it back. If I'd never spilled the beans on My Dear's boyfriend, she would have kept me.

I pulled into my assigned parking space and dried my eyes with napkins left from my last rendezvous with McDonald's. Then I looked in the rearview mirror. My eyes were red and swollen. Dried tears made a trail to my chin. Lucky for me, I didn't wear makeup or streaks of mascara stains would've decorated my face instead. With both hands on the steering wheel, I leaned my head back and closed my eyes. Once again, I took a couple of deep breaths to gain my composure. I gathered myself, then smiled. At least my son would know his father. He wouldn't have to spend his life dreaming about a relationship that would never exist. Not knowing me wouldn't affect him because I'm not worthy of his love.

I opened my eyes and cursed to myself when I noticed a money green Nissan Altima parked across the street directly in front of my apartment building. Fire erupted from my ears. Jared always found a way to piss me off and today was no different. I had asked him a million times in a million ways to call before he came to my apartment. Why was this fool inside of my house when I was not home, especially when I was not due home for another couple of hours? I walked into the apartment slowly, not really wanting to face Jared. All I wanted to do was have a glass of my favorite wine and allow my thoughts to keep me company. I stood in the doorway of my bedroom, staring at the bed. Lying there, on top of the covers, barefoot, and comfortably sleeping was Jared.

"Hey!"

Jared rolled over so fast he fell off the edge of the bed, onto the floor.

"Hey, baby! What are you doing home? I figured you would be at the office for a while."

"Well, actually I should be asking what you're doing here. I live here, or did you forget?"

I walked away before Jared could respond. I wanted to ask him how he got in but I knew he'd used the spare key I'd kept hidden for emergencies.

"Damn," I mumbled, shaking my head. The last thing I wanted was to be dealing with Jared, but the first thing I wanted was a glass of wine. There was nothing like a good, stiff drink when he was bugging me.

He followed me into the living area then over to the bar where he sat on the edge of a stool looking goofy. Things became a little uncomfortable when we made eye contact. I was starting to feel as if he could read my mind. Finally, he looked away, struggling to keep his eyes off me. I calmed myself before speaking. After all, it wasn't really Jared's fault I was in a foul mood. The combination of Mrs. Young's visit and my constant thoughts about Omar were taking their toll on me.

I sighed heavily before speaking, "Um baby, I think we're way overdue for a nice evening together. What do you say we go out for dinner and drinks tonight? Your choice, my treat."

Jared accepted my invitation so I asked him to meet me back at my apartment around six, which was my way of getting rid of him without being rude. Now I would have a few hours to take a nap like I had come home to do with enough time left to freshen up before dinner.

The ringing of my doorbell jarred me from the dreams of Omar that were dancing around in my head, taking over my sleep. I pried my eyes open, stretched, yawned, and searched around for my cell phone so I could look at it for the time. It was six o'clock. I knew it was Jared at the door because he, unlike all of the other brothers I have encountered, was always on time. The doorbell rang again, this time at the same time my cell phone began to buzz.

"Jared, Jared, Jared," I mumbled to myself as I crawled toward the door.

The doorbell rang again.

"Coming!" I yelled.

When I opened the door, Jared stood there looking fine as wine, and I love me some wine. He was so sexy in his button-down polo shirt and slacks. I liked Jared because he had a versatile fashion sense. Omar would have shown up in some hood gear. I smiled at

Jared, running my fingers through my tangled mane, trying to pretend I was getting dressed.

"What took you so long to answer the door?" Jared asked after I finished checking him out.

"I was in the back trying to find an outfit. Come in. I'll be dressed in a flash," I lied.

"You need to quit lying. If I know you as well as I think I do, you were asleep, but it's all good. Get dressed; we have plenty of time. I picked a nice place, you will have a blast." He laughed and tapped me on the butt as I walked away. I heard Omar close the door behind him. Did I say Omar? I meant, Jared. You see, the problem is that whenever Omar consumed my thoughts, I always confused their names. My biggest fear is that I will make that same mistake when I'm talking to Jared. That's a costly slip-up. I hope it never happens.

Kimberlee

Big Doc had become even more distant lately. He'd always been busy, but somewhere along the course of this marriage, lines had been crossed.

Shontay's attitude toward me was more volatile, yet she smothered my husband with her attention. Like a genie, his wish was her every command. Even worse, I was starting to feel like her Facebook statuses were directed at me.

It had been a while since Big Doc spent any time with me. He was always busy. He never had time to steal away with me--, his wife, once the woman of his dreams.

Some mornings I would wake early to catch him before he left for the day. All I wanted was a simple breakfast. Instead I would get a chance to see him with Shontay and a breakfast she'd cooked, a breakfast they would share together. He talked. She laughed. It almost seemed intimate. Like something was happening right under my nose. I was sick of watching Shontay sashay around my home, pilfering intimate moments with my husband, taking time that belonged to me. I can't take it anymore, she's out of here, but first I have to find her replacement, preferably an old, unattractive woman, or maybe a man who could serve me like Shontay had been doing my husband.

I decided to call my mother. I wanted to talk to her about firing Shontay. It was amazing how much control she still had over my life. I realized a long time ago she treated me like a child, but I allowed it because I loved my mother with all of me. There wasn't one thing on this Earth that my mother wouldn't do for me, and she'd proved it repeatedly. Sometimes she went to the extreme, but that's because her love was extreme.

"Hello."

"Mama, it's me."

"Hey Pumpkin, what a pleasant surprise. I haven't talked to you in a couple of days, and I sure have missed my baby. How have you been?"

"I'm good, mama. Things couldn't be better." I couldn't tell my mother that my marriage was lonely. I still loved my husband, and I didn't want him hurt. The whole point of this call was for her permission to get rid of Shontay.

I continued, "I have one slight problem I need your help with. Maybe you can give me some advice."

"Anything for you. You know Mama will always have your back. You're my only baby."

"I know. That's why I called you."

"What's wrong?"

I wasn't sure how to tell her. My mother had been on my back so long about giving Shontay a chance. She didn't like to be wrong about anything so I had to be careful in my approach. I didn't want her to feel like she was being second guessed.

"Well, there's a problem with Shontay. I'm not sure how to say this but I think she's trying to steal my husband."

"Don't be silly, Kimberlee. First of all, your husband would never go for someone like her. You're insulting yourself if you believe she has a chance. Second, I'm sure Shontay knows not to even go there." She slightly chuckled.

Honestly, I didn't see the humor in the situation. I've been noticing things between that tramp and my husband and I'm sure something is going on. After all, I wasn't the purest woman when he chose me.

"I'm serious. Something is up with them, Mama. I want to get rid of her. She's no longer welcome in my home."

"Listen to your mama, honey. Eddie Lee would never stoop so low. He's working a lot; you're probably paranoid. I tell you what, you should keep an eye on Shontay. Meanwhile, make your husband remember why he chose you. Prepare a nice, romantic dinner, feed his stomach and his ego, make him feel as if he's the only man on the planet. Men want to feel desired like women do. I guarantee you things will improve between the two of you."

"I never said we were having problems. I said Shontay wants him," I answered defensively.

"You didn't have to tell me there are problems. If everything was peachy, there would be no cause for alarm with Shontay. It's obvious. Remember, Mama wasn't born last night. Now, as I was saying, make your husband feel like the man he is. Remind him why he chose you to be his wife, and things will smooth out. If you do that, then Shontay is no issue. We'll decide what to do about her later. For now, get your husband back."

"Yes ma'am." I was disappointed; I wanted Shontay gone ASAP but I didn't want to upset my mama.

"Remember that I love you. I'm only an hour away and can be there in a snap if you need me."

"I love you, too."

I disconnected the phone feeling worse than I did before I called. My mother had a point. There was a strain on my marriage, and I was going crazy. I had to take action. I called a local barbecue restaurant and asked them to prepare a meal for two. It wasn't the most romantic dinner, but my man loves ribs.

Eddie Lee came home late in the evening. I was upstairs in the bedroom when I heard him enter the kitchen through the garage. I stayed away from the mall today and sent Shontay home early. I didn't want her to be in my house when my husband arrived from work. I needed alone time with Big Doc and I didn't want her anywhere on his mind during my time. The barbecue place had delivered our meal and I'd set up our cherry wood kitchen table with a beautiful place setting for two.

I rushed down the stairs in a sexy, purple and black satin number with sheer, see-through sides that I'd ordered online from Frederick's of Hollywood.

"Hey you," I said, grinning from ear to ear, truly happy to see my man.

"Hi." He spoke dryly, walking past me as if I were nobody to him. He didn't even notice my lingerie.

I was disappointed, not surprised. Our relationship had been deteriorating for a while, but I honestly hadn't noticed or cared until recently. Most women were blinded by love. I was blinded by credit cards and shopping. Watching Shontay's interest in my husband helped alleviate my loss of sight. Before she waltzed into our lives, I could go days without seeing him as long as I had access to his black American Express card. That plastic addiction funded the shopping sprees that gave me "Red Bottoms", Manolo Blahnik and Jimmy Choo pumps, Fendi dresses, Louis Vuitton, Gucci, and DKNY everything else. I didn't care if he ever spoke to me as long as I was able to feed my addiction. In my opinion, my attitude was Big Doc's fault. He paid to get me so he had to pay to keep me. I don't make the rules; I just follow them.

I tried to ignore his lack of enthusiasm at seeing me, and reached to wrap my arms around his waist when I was close enough to him. He sighed, showing his annoyance, and pulled away from me, a second indication that our marriage was in trouble.

A wave of desolation flooded my body when I realized he wasn't feeling me, but I didn't give up. I'm a diva. No one resists me. I always get what I want.

My third attempt at getting my husband's attention was more desperate. I reached again, this time for his zipper. Mama used to tell me that the way to a man's heart is his stomach. My college experiences taught me a better way. Big Doc looked at me with exasperation, but he didn't pull away. I unbuttoned his pants right there in the kitchen and pushed him back against the marble counter-top. I then dropped to my knees to take care of my business. Resistance gone, he put both of his hands on my head as it bobbed up and down. A parade of umms marched from his mouth as I took him to that place. My mission was to remind him who I was and why he married me. Once he reached his peak, his expression changed from ultimate pleasure to utter disgust. Big Doc pulled his pants up and stared at me.

"Get up! You are pitiful. You should be ashamed and embarrassed," he said, walking around me toward the stairs that would lead him to the guest bedroom where he'd been sleeping.

My ego was bruised. I didn't have the energy to fight with him. My plan to make amends left me with my tail between my legs. I extinguished the candles and put the food away. I didn't have much of an appetite after such blatant rejection. Alicia repeatedly told Tomeka to get a vibrator to ward off her lonely feeling. Looks like I'm the one who needs the help.

I retreated to my lavishly laid bedroom into my California-King sized bed. I pulled the goose down comforter up to my neck and stared at the ceiling. The past came falling down toward me.

Big Doc and I met in college. I was running through men like a track meet. I didn't consider myself a slut. I had to do what I had to do to get what I needed to get. Big Doc chased me like I was the last woman on Earth. Ironically, I wasn't the least bit interested in him and wouldn't have had him if he was the last man on Earth. He shadowed me for months, asking me out. I constantly turned him down. He didn't deserve me. I was too fine for his type. Eventually someone told him what he needed to do to get with me. To this day, I don't know how he found out, but I'm glad he did. He came at me proper, told me he was going to be a doctor and that he came from a family of doctors. My interest was especially piqued when he began to treat me to expensive lunches and dinners. After that, he was paying to get my hair and nails done. The day he bought my first pair of Manolo pumps, he had me hooked. All of that before I ever spread eagle for him. He just wanted me, and that's what he paid for.

I shook my head thinking about how times had changed. Instead of Big Doc chasing me, I was now chasing him. After enduring the night of rejection, I called Shontay before the crack of dawn and told her not to bother coming to work for a while. I didn't terminate her employment. I gave her time off with pay. I couldn't stand the sight of her because my heart kept telling me she was the cause of my man's behavior. He smiled at her and talked to her more in a few minutes than he did with me over the course of a week. I couldn't take it.

The next day, I spent the entire day pampering myself. I started at the spa, getting the full treatment: a full-body massage, a facial, and both a manicure and pedicure. I even tried that new vaginal steaming that all the reality stars are raving about.

Next, I headed to one of the most expensive restaurants in town, simply because I felt like it. Last, but not least, I hit the mall, spending over six thousand dollars all on me and my babies.

Fortunately, Alicia called and invited me to Mary Love's before I could do anymore spending. I couldn't have been more ready for a glass of wine, and like Tomeka a chance to live vicariously through Alicia's sex life. Alicia got on my nerves going on and on about that good for nothing man of hers. I was so jealous, it was hard to hide. I decided then and there this gathering would be my last encounter at Mary Love's. Frankly, I was tired of everyone. I just needed time to myself.

Tomeka

It was Sunday morning and I was up getting ready for church. I'd kept my word to myself and God this time. I'd been attending every worship service faithfully and taking the boys with me. Malik hadn't changed much. He was still hustling and I didn't even ask him to go to church.

Right now, he was cooking breakfast for himself and the boys to eat while I was gone. Normally, I would take them with me but for some reason, Malik wanted them to stay with him today. I didn't object because although he loved them and gave them the world, he didn't spend a lot of quality time with them. In fact, I'm not sure Malik could define quality time. I had every pair of Nikes that existed. My bedroom was basically a boutique and I had a bank account full of money. My man has me pushing a Porsche Cayenne, but I can't tell you the last time he's taken me out. I can't tell you the last time he even talked about taking me out for that matter.

"I'm leaving. I'll be back in a few hours," I said to Malik before closing the front door.

I was barely out the driveway when my cell phone was ringing. It was Malik.

"Hey, babe, stop by the market on your way home to pick up some meat. I wanna barbecue."

"Yes, daddy," I stated sarcastically.

After church, I stopped by the hospital to visit Tyler, the gunshot victim. Thoughts of him wouldn't escape me. They nagged at me constantly- I couldn't shake them. Tyler was like a brother to me because he saw me every day for the first thirty days after his injury. I brought food, flowers, movies, and lots of prayer as he fought to live. I wanted nothing more than a full recovery for him. He was the sweetest young man with a brilliant future ahead of him. Tyler was a medical student. His dream was to save the world. You'd never meet another Tyler in all your life because he was a one of a kind dude.

"Well Tyler, it was good seeing you again today. You are always such a pleasure to be around. I hope you enjoy the pepperoni pizza; I know it's your favorite."

"Thanks Tomeka. I hate this hospital food. I'd probably starve if it wasn't for you." Tyler laughed, taking a slice of pizza.

"Anything for you Tyler. I want you up and out of here as soon as possible," I said.

"I think it's going to take a lot more than pizza to get me out of this place. It's going to take an act of God. It's scary but I know He'll bring me through. I'm going to be a minister when I overcome this situation. It's my testimony."

I smiled at Tyler. He was tugging at my heart strings, just as he always did.

"And you're part of that blessing, Tomeka. I know you can find other things to do with your time. I can't for the life of me figure out why you're here with me so much. My sister hasn't been here for me like you have. In fact, she's only visited me twice. Why do you come?"

I rubbed Tyler's arm but I didn't speak. I didn't have an answer for him. He asked me all the time why I came and I never had an answer. I made a deal with God to save Tyler and I wanted to be there to witness the miracle. For Tyler to survive, all I had to do was live a Christian life and that's what I would do. Part of being a Christian was upholding my part of the bargain, and that involved looking out for Tyler.

"You don't have to answer me Tomeka, I understand." He rubbed my hand in return.

No matter when I came, Tyler always asked me why before I left. It was a ritual. I left his room, headed to my car. I didn't want to leave, but I had to. Malik was home waiting for me to bring groceries for a cookout and Lord knows he'd have a hissy fit if I didn't show up on time. It was weird how the thought of Malik could change my mood so fast. He was so selfish. He'd even accused me of having a crush on Tyler. He couldn't have been more off base.

"Hello, Tomeka!" A familiar voice called my name.

I looked up to see Kimberlee's husband, Eddie Lee walking toward me.

"Hey there Eddie Lee," I smiled as he approached me. "Fancy meeting you here."

He leaned in to give me a hug. "I know, right. I'm only a doctor. What would I be doing at a hospital?"

"Well, you know what I mean," I said, playfully nudging his arm.

"Yea Tomeka, I know what you mean. So how's Tyler? I'm sure you're here visiting him."

"Wow Eddie Lee. Do I come that much?"

"You're here a lot, but it's admirable of you."

I'm sure I was blushing. That was a flattering comment, especially coming from someone as smart as Eddie Lee.

"Thanks Eddie Lee, how nice of you. I guess I'd better be going. Malik's going to barbecue today so I've got to stop by the grocery store on the way home."

"Well then, I'll talk to you later. It's always good to see you. In fact, I'd love to see you anytime. Take my number."

Eddie Lee handed me a business card. I took it without a second thought, then moved quickly away. I didn't like where this was going, but I'd keep the number…just in case I needed it.

"Goodbye."

Seeing Eddie Lee opened the flood gates and thoughts of our encounter at my birthday party drowned me. Kimberlee was blessed to have such a wonderful man in her life. If I had a man like him, I'd definitely appreciate being able to enjoy his money without the fear of losing him to jail because of it. I made a mental note to remind Kimberlee of her good fortune the very next time she was around.

Once home, I brought in ribs, chicken, and hot dogs for Malik to grill and made a beeline to the bathroom before he could ask me to help. Hidden in an aspirin bottle in the medicine cabinet was a joint I had rolled the night before. I took it out, then turned on the bathroom fan and the shower to reduce the smell of smoke before I took my first drag.

I'd changed enormously. I didn't drink, smoke cigarettes, or cuss. In addition, I tried not to lie but there was something about that Mary Jane I couldn't shake. My occasional smoke became a basic daily need. It helped maintain my sanity while dealing with Malik. He was driving me insane. One day I loved him. The next day I hated him. Like I said, there's a thin line between love and hate. I guess that means I will stop hating him the same day I stop loving him. If that's the case, I'll hate him forever.

I relit my funny cigarette to get one last hit before I showered and changed out of my church attire. The moment it touched my lips there was a knock on the bathroom door. I took a deep breath before responding.

"What?"

"Hurry up," Malik said, being a little too chipper for me.

"Go to the other bathroom. The benefit of having three bathrooms is no one has to be rushed. I'm trying to take a shower."

I answered him with a bit of annoyance. He always wanted to tell me what to do, which is why I needed to smoke. He would make a truly sane man go mad.

"Come out. Don't drown. I want you to peel the potatoes and make a potato salad."

"I thought he said he was doing all the cooking," I mumbled under my breath.

"Meka!"

"I'm coming, baby," I said in another attempt to keep the peace. I killed the weed, took a sixty-second shower, and headed to the kitchen.

"I thought you said you were doing all the cooking," I said when he handed me the bag of potatoes.

"Woman, are you saying that you can't even peel the potatoes for me? I *AM* doing all the cooking. All I want you to do is peel the potatoes, and you can't do that. Come on Meka, work with me. Peel the potatoes, baby, and don't complain." He looked at me out the side of his eyes.

"I'm not complaining. All I'm saying is whenever I do all the cooking every day, you don't peel a potato. If you're going to give me a break, give me a break, don't ask for my help."

I wasn't backing down.

Malik was finally annoyed. I could hear it in his voice.

"And you have the nerve to wonder why I don't ever stay home. This is the stuff I have to put up with. I try to do something nice for you and it's not enough. It's never enough, Meka. No matter what I do, it's never enough. You talked all that smack last night. 'Malik never stays home. Malik won't take me out. Malik doesn't spend any time with the boys.' So what did Malik do for the same Tomeka who begs him to be here but won't give him no play? He kept the boys home while you went to church so you could enjoy services without having to keep an eye on them. He even decided to make dinner so you wouldn't have to, and what does he get in return? This bullshit! You're seriously pissing me off."

"I'm pissing you off, Malik? Well, how about this? I will answer your question for you. It will be enough when it doesn't have to be a special occasion for you to spend time with the family. It will be enough when you don't deserve accolades for doing things you should want to do. It will be enough when you help me because you want to and not because I cried last night, Malik. It will be enough when it's sincere. You're doing this because I asked you to and not because you want to. The question is not when will it be enough. The question is when will you get it?"

I stormed out of the kitchen back to the bedroom. Malik followed me closely.

"Wait a minute. Don't walk away now. Last night you were crying because I wasn't here, now you're crying because I am. I don't have time for this. You're confused, not me, you can figure it out alone. I'm leaving!"

This time he stormed out and I followed him.

"That's right, leave now Malik. Run away from me like you always do. That's what you want to do anyway. All you needed was an excuse, so go! Leave, but this time, don't come back. I hate you, Malik." Tears spewed out like a shaken soda pop.

"You're right. I'm leaving. All I needed was an excuse, and you just gave me one. I'm leaving but remember you asked for this, not me." Malik turned and went back into the bedroom. He went to the closet and grabbed an overnight bag then started rummaging through all of the drawers. He stuffed the bag while I watched him. Neither of us spoke another word.

Once it quieted down, Khalil and Khalik peeked around the corner. They started crying because I was crying.

"Where is Daddy going, Mommy?" They whined in unison.

I pulled both of them onto my lap before speaking. Seeing them cry was tearing me apart. Maybe this would be Malik's wake-up call. He had never left me like this before, especially with the boys looking on. They continued to ask why their dad was leaving. Malik didn't speak, he continued to pack with an ice-cold look.

"Where is Daddy going?" Khalil asked me again.

"I don't know son. You have to ask Daddy," I answered, looking up at Malik.

"Where are you going, Daddy?" Khalik cried.

Silence engulfed the room. I stopped crying because I wanted to hear the answer Malik would come up with. He stopped packing for a second and stared at each of the boys.

"Come to Daddy, guys." Malik sat on the edge of the bed and put each of them on one knee. He grabbed their chins, making them look him directly in the eyes. They all looked seriously solemn. He kissed them both on the forehead, looking into their eyes once more before he spoke.

"Daddy is going to get some space right now. I'm going to go take a time-out. You know how sometimes you guys fight and Mommy and I make you take a time out in separate rooms? Well Daddy and Mommy are taking a time-out."

A self-certified street hustler, yet he was so in love with his sons. That's the side of him that I'd grown to love. He had a soft spot for our babies.

"Okay," Khalil said cheerfully as he jumped down from Malik's lap, walking toward me.

Khalik was still a bit more taken aback. He hung on to Malik's neck. "Don't leave us Daddy, we'll be good."

Khalil skipped over to his ten-minute younger brother, and grabbed his hand.

"Don't cry Bubba. Daddy's not leaving. He's taking a time-out in the other room. He's not mad at us. He's mad at Mommy. Daddy would never leave us."

Khalik didn't let go of his Daddy's neck. He used both of his hands to make Malik look him square in the eyes. "Is he right Daddy? Are you going to stay in a different room? Are you mad at Mommy, not us?"

"I wouldn't leave you guys for a million bucks," he answered.

Malik's body slumped. His eyes reflected defeat. I knew he wanted to leave, but he took his bag of clothes into the guest bedroom with the boys hot on his trail.

"You can put your stuff in this drawer, Daddy," I heard Khalil say in his usually chipper voice. The boys were happy as long as their hero was staying. I wish I could say the same for me.

While they followed Malik around soaking up all of the newfound attention they were getting, I went back to the bathroom and relit my joint. I would just have to take another shower afterward.

I smoked until I didn't have a care in the world, then took a long, hot bath. My body needed the attention. I spent so much time trying to please my three men I'd totally neglected myself. When I was done in the tub, I dressed in the pink and white Nike jumper Malik had recently gifted me with, then left the house.

I didn't bother telling Malik I was leaving. He should be able to watch the boys for the day and I would have the day to myself. I didn't really have a destination in mind so I called my friend Tina, from church.

Tina was a cool girl. She couldn't replace my buddy, Alicia but she was pretty close. Alicia and I had been friends throughout our childhood, but I'd recently met Tina at a church function. She was coming out of a traumatic experience and so was I. The same event took both of us to church that Sunday. It saved our lives and brought us together as sisters. Tina and I clicked instantly. We were around the same age with the same interests. I'd never met another chick who had so many similarities to me as she did.

When I found out she was a closet smoker, like me, our friendship blossomed. No one knew either of us smoked so when we were not "closet" smoking alone, we were doing it together. My other friends thought I could do no wrong, and I sincerely tried not to but smoking was my weakness.

One day Tina and I talked about what led us looking to change our lives. I told her about the guy who was shot in my driveway in the middle of the night. She told me that her younger brother had been shot on the same night, at the same time, at the same address. We cried together. As it turns out, Tyler was Tina's brother. When we met at church, her face was familiar to me because I'd seen her at the hospital. Our bond was sealed through tragedy. No one would ever make me believe God didn't put Tina in my life for a reason.

"Hey friend," she sang, answering her cell phone on the first ring.

"Hey girl," I answered, not sounding as chipper.

"Uh-oh. What's wrong?" Her friend radar kicked in. "Let me guess. It's Malik. Come on over, I will get the closet ready." She laughed.

"I'm on your block," I said.

Not long after we hung up the phone, I hid my sorrows behind a cloud of smoke. I cried a little as I told Tina about my argument with Malik.

"Malik is such a punk. He just doesn't get it, does he?"

I gave her an ugly look. In my mind, no one could talk bad about Malik but me.

"You better watch your mouth girl, that's still my man! I'm the only person who can call him a punk."

"I can't believe you're defending him! Okay, Meka, go ahead and take up for him but if you're going to do that then you need to stop driving over here to cry on my shoulder. I'm sick of hearing about the women on his Facebook page, and I'm sick of hearing about how he's never at home. Do something about it or be miserable, that's up to you. I know one thing though, I couldn't be you. You're a good girl. Don't let Malik bring you down. He's only doing what you allow him to do. If you would put your foot down, you wouldn't go through this. See, Malik couldn't handle a chick like me. You're soft; he can treat you like garbage and get away with it."

Tina had gotten on her soap box. She was always preaching to me about Malik even though she didn't have a man of her own. She hated him and was always quick to point it out. I listened to her go on for another hour, telling me about Malik. During that hour, I noticed that her cell was ringing off the hook. She kept silencing it. Finally, when it rang again, I told her that she should answer the phone because I was about to leave anyway.

She waved her hands and rolled her eyes at the phone, "He'll call back. He always does."

"Who is it?" I asked nosily. I didn't see a problem with it because she was always in my business.

"Just some punk," she said.

We both laughed.

I stood up to leave before it hit me that I didn't have anywhere to go. I didn't want to go home yet, and I didn't want to see Alicia while I was buzzing so I decided I was going to chill with Tina a while longer.

"What are you doing?" She asked when I sat back down.

"I need to let this buzz wear off so I'm going to hang around here for a minute more."

She seemed disappointed that I wasn't leaving, which was weird because she'd never refused my company. Normally, it was her idea for me to stay longer.

"I'll leave," I said slightly annoyed.

"No, don't leave. It's cool," she stuttered.

I wasn't comfortable with Tina's answer, but I hung around her place simply to keep from going home. I didn't want to be in the house with Malik.

I leaned back in my seat and rubbed my face. The weed was getting to me. I was getting hungry and sleepy.

Right in the nick of time my cell rang. It was Alicia asking me to meet her and Kimberlee at Mary Love's for drinks.

I used to love our girls' nights, but because I'd been trying to live a Christian lifestyle, I felt out of place at Mary Love's. Before the shooting, I would have been in the mix, drinking with my girls, then going home to get with my man. Those were the best nights. When we go out now, I secretly covet their drinks, all the while wishing I could smoke, and listen to the stories about their sex lives. Do you know how hard it is to watch them get drunk without joining in the fun? Despite my apprehension, I told Alicia I'd be there. After all, Tina was acting shady, and I didn't want to go home.

Tomeka

Malik was waiting for me when I strolled in from Mary Love's. I didn't feel like dealing with his mess so I walked past him as if I didn't see him. The joint in the medicine cabinet was calling me to the bathroom. I'd planned to smoke, shower, and go to bed. Malik, however, had other plans.

"Where have you been all day, Tomeka?" he said obviously agitated.

"What? I know you're not questioning me, Mr. Never Come Home. Why do you care where I've been? Aren't you leaving?" I said, not missing a step.

"Don't play games with me, girl. I'm not up for your bull tonight. Where have you been?"

"Shhhhh," I said more aggravated than he was. "Why are you yelling anyway? You could wake the boys!"

"You haven't been worried about the boys all day so don't start that fake shit. Where were you?" He asked again, following me into the bathroom.

I turned on the shower, removed my clothes, and stepped under the warm flow of water, hoping Malik would go away. He was bugging me. I wanted to smoke before taking a shower but he'd ruined that for me. Malik pulled the shower curtain back to inform me the conversation wasn't over before he walked out of the bathroom, slamming the door. I couldn't have been more excited. I stepped out of the shower, with the water still running and smoked myself into oblivion.

My wheels immediately began to spin out of control. Malik was driving me insane. I loved the hell out of him, but I was tired of the pointless, stupid arguments. If Malik wanted to leave me, I was cool with it. I could handle myself. Unlike Malik, I'd gone to college and got a degree in accounting. Besides, Malik had a savings account in my name that was fifty thousand dollars strong, enough to last until I could find a job. As a matter of fact, I had access to all of Malik's money. He gave me access so I could get to the money if something happened to him.

The more I thought about our relationship, being with Malik became less and less appealing. Each day that passed made it easier not to be intimate with him. I wanted to find me a nice, Christian man who would understand my views on church. Malik was not even halfway there. In fact, besides the boys, Malik didn't care about anything but money. I didn't want to think about Malik anymore. I wished I could wash the day's events from me. No matter how hard I scrubbed, it didn't cleanse me like I wanted to be cleansed. I kept hearing Malik tell me he was leaving me and I couldn't get the vision of him packing from my mind. If the twins hadn't intervened, Malik would have left. I was tired of him, so I had to do something about it.

Alicia

My date with Jared was unbelievable. He'd gotten tickets for us to see my favorite R&B artist, Ashley Washington perform live at Club Platinum Rose. I spent the night singing and swaying to her soulful sound. Ashley hadn't quite made the big time yet, but she was well on her way. Anytime there was an event in the city, Ashley was our go to chic for singing. She has the talent; her voice is heavenly. Jared said with the right management team, Ashley would blow the top off the charts. After several encores, the deejay took over and we partied until the club closed.

Jared and I ended up at my place. I wanted to call Kimberlee to tell her how perfect my night had been. It was three in the morning so I decided to wait. Besides this would be our reason to get together for drinks.

Jared disappeared to the back room while I poured two glasses of wine. We were both in love with the Riesling Omar had introduced me to. Jared returned to the living room motioning for me to follow him. I held up drinks, and he made his way over to me. He grabbed his glass from my hands, raising it to the air.

"To us," he said.

"To us," I repeated.

He grabbed both my hands and wrapped my arms around his waist, leading me into the bedroom. The scent of vanilla permeated the air, telling me candles were lit all around before I ever saw them. Silk rose petals adorned my bed. I could hear the trickle of water sliding into the whirlpool tub. We made our way into the bathroom to the whirlpool.

"Let's take this to the bed," Jared said, gently helping me out of the tub.

My entire body tingled, seeing him in nothing but a towel had me full of anticipation. He took the time to dry me off before he flipped me onto the bed. He planted kisses up and down my back. I could barely stand it. He turned me over, pressing his juicy wet lips to mine. I pulled him closer to me. I wanted to feel his nature rise, I wanted him inside me, but Jared didn't grant my wish right away. He scooped me up by the legs and put his entire face in my pot of honey. My body shook. Finally, he put his key in my lock and our bodies meshed into one, as we rocked passionately to a rhythm created by our souls. I couldn't move when it was over. For the first time in our relationship, Jared had scratched that itch for me.

My excitement about the night I'd spent with Jared brought me and the girls to Mary Love's the next day. I'd called each one of them, asking them to meet me for drinks. Mary Love's was crawling with its regular patrons. We'd been coming in for years so the owner always personally served our drinks. He brought over a Magnotta Riesling Ice Wine for me and Kimberlee, and water for Tomeka, who normally drank margaritas, but not since she'd been going to church.

I started the conversation. "You ladies are not going to believe what I have to say."

"What are you waiting for? Fill us in," Tomeka said taking a sip from her water, fanning herself with her hands.

"Jared finally gave me an orgasm."

A chorus of wows, laughter, and high-fives followed that statement.

Tomeka spoke again, "Oh no missy, you're not getting off that easy. We want details. This celibacy thing is kicking my butt."

They hung on my every word as I described my perfect night with Jared. If I didn't know better, I would have thought I noticed a tinge of jealousy in Kimberlee's eyes. She tried to be happy for me but something was obviously wrong.

While they continued the banter, I excused myself to the bathroom. The three glasses of wine had taken their toll on me. I felt the effects of the alcohol as I staggered toward the entrance to the restroom. I hovered over the toilet and held the door with my foot. I'd had to pee so bad I didn't have a chance to latch the lock. The stall door flung open as soon as I stood to zip my pants. I stood upright, holding my shirt under my chin as I fastened my jeans. I caught a glimpse of myself in the mirror and immediately dropped my blouse to cover the scars that were permanently etched in my skin, a constant reminder of the man who'd put them there. I left the bathroom with Omar on my mind.

I did my best to cover my angst. I didn't want to ruin the girls' night that I'd called so I put on a happy face. When I returned to the table, the live band had started its performance so my girls were in a zone. The crooning of the all-male band swept away any thoughts of Omar. Before I knew it, I was on my feet rocking to the music. Kimberlee sauntered onto the makeshift dance floor next to me. She had a glass of wine in each hand and tried to pass one off to me.

"No way, honey. I'm already tipsy. Give that drink to someone who needs it," I said not losing a beat.

I kept dancing but Kimberlee went back to her seat.

The wine eventually got the best of me. I said a quick round of goodbyes before I headed out the door, with my cell attached to my ear, calling Jared.

I was too tired to go in to work Monday morning. I didn't realize how late it was when I left Mary Love's. I stayed up even later waiting for Jared to return my calls. Yes, I said calls. I'd called him three times before leaving a voicemail. It was unlike Jared to ignore me. Then again, I'd never called him so late because I'd never been horny and yearning to be with Jared. He'd never given me a reason to long for him, however, our last encounter was one I wanted to relive. I waited up all night but he never called or stopped by. I didn't know whether to be worried or upset.

When Jared called later the next day, I wasn't enthused.

"What's up baby?"

"Are you ok, Jared?" I asked sincerely.

I didn't want to go off on him based on an assumption so I asked to be sure. Jared told me flat out that he was asleep when I called and changed the subject. It irritated me to be dismissed like that but I didn't want to argue with him over something so trivial so I kept my mouth shut. He told me he had to go to work and he'd stop by after he got off. I hung up the phone without a word. My insides were boiling. I wanted to yell, scream, and cuss but the words wouldn't come out. My mouth had stopped but my mind was racing. Something was strange with Jared's behavior. I had to get to the bottom of his sudden change.

Kimberlee

I couldn't shake the fact that my husband rejected my advances toward him. Things were worse than I thought. He'd never been blatantly disrespectful to me. It seemed like things were going farther down the toilet, spiraling out of control like the tidy bowl man in his toilet tornado. I'd spent many days frustrated and looking for answers. Big Doc had never refused my oral pleasure. He always said I had the best mouth in the south, yet he was able to resist. My heart beat out of control. Something was telling me our relationship was over. I needed to know for sure.

I logged into my Facebook account, and clicked on my husband's profile searching for clues. It didn't take long before I saw Shontay's comments all over his page. She was full of compliments and smiley faces. She had the nerve to tell him how handsome he was on one of his pictures. I was fit to be tied. At this point, I didn't give a damn what anybody said. Today would be Shontay's last day on the job. I was sure if Mama knew about Shontay's Facebook compliments to Big Doc, she'd agree with me. In addition to firing Shontay, I would confront my husband as soon as he came home.

I called my mama to talk to her about what was going on in my mind. She pissed me off for the first time in forever. Although she agreed with me that Shontay's actions in my home and on

Facebook were an indication of something fishy, she wanted me to accept it and move on. She told me he was probably getting a little something on the side like my dad had but said it wasn't a big deal. Mama had me messed up, there was no way I'd accept him getting nookie on the side. I was convinced he was cheating and determined to confront him. I refused to be treated the same way my mother had. I told my mama I would call her back, before I said something I'd later regret.

I sat in the great room on the sofa for hours cuddling my babies, tears flowing, waiting for Eddie Lee to walk through the door. My poodles were always comforting. Without a shadow of doubt, I knew they loved me unconditionally.

A knock on the front door startled me. I wasn't expecting any company. Both Roxi and Sabri barked incessantly at the door. None of us were in the mood for company. The peephole was covered so I walked over and looked out the window. It was Alicia. I shook my head. I didn't feel like being bothered. I almost walked away without answering the door. Instead, I stepped back, took a deep breath, and put on a happy face.

Alicia walked in prying in my business. She didn't ask any questions, just gave me that look. The same look she'd used to make me spill the beans since we were kids. I didn't appreciate her unannounced presence but I needed to talk, so I told her everything. She gave me an outlet and a different perspective. She watched me pack my things. I'd reached the end of my rope and was leaving. Alicia left and I waited for my husband to come home.

As soon as the garage whirred open, I marched down the stairs. This time there was no dinner, no negligee, and no romance. This was strictly a confrontation. When the door flung open, I was there with my hands on my hips. Big Doc walked in. I stood glaring at him for a while.

"Why the hell are you standing there like that? Who are you supposed to be?"

I stood my ground. I didn't say a word, just stared at him trying to grab some strength from his anger. Why did he have an attitude? I was the one being lied to and cheated on. I was point blank with him. No holds barred. "Are you cheating on me?"

"Don't start. I've had a long day." His face made it known that he wasn't in the mood.

"I asked you a question, Eddie Lee. Are you cheating on me?"

"Don't ask questions you really don't want to know the answers to."

He was so matter of fact, he was making me sick, yet I didn't back down.

"I won't. Are you cheating on me?"

"Yes," he nodded without regret.

My hand flew over my mouth. It felt like the wind was being sucked from me, but he walked away casually as if he hadn't shattered my world. I chased him up the stairs.

"Why?"

He kept walking.

I pounded his back with my fists. "Why? Why?"

"You've been cheating on me for years. I can't believe you're going to stand here and pretend like you care about me."

"I've never had a thought about cheating on you!" I was screaming to the top of my lungs.

"You've had an affair with my money for years, Kimberlee. You've never loved me. It's always been about the money for you." He kept his composure, obviously not shaken by anything that was happening.

I dropped my head because he was right. It hurt to hear him say it, though.

"Who is she?"

"Doesn't matter."

"We can make this work."

"Are you willing to have my baby?"

A look of panic struck my face. It was no secret I didn't want children. I didn't have an answer because I didn't want to lie to him.

He spoke again before I could think of what to say next, "She's willing to have my baby."

"Okay. If you end the affair, I will bear the burden of a baby."

"Do you mean it?" he grinned. "Let's get started tonight!"

Big Doc literally swept me off my feet and carried me the rest of the way up the stairs to our bedroom as if he didn't hear me say the word "burden".

Alicia

I couldn't put my finger on where my relationship with Jared was going. Things were good, but I sensed change. I couldn't figure out whether the changes were good or bad. All I knew for sure is things were changing. I didn't pressure Jared about it. I'm sure he recognized it without me pointing it out. Besides, I didn't want to push him away. It was almost like our relationship was at a standstill because I didn't want to show any emotion. There's just something about letting a man know that you love him that confuses the relationship. Somewhere along the way, he realizes that your love for him is a weakness and he takes advantage of it. That's exactly what happened between me and Omar. I told him I loved him and he put me down like four flat tires.

Hmph, Omar. Forget him.

I decided to take my cousin, Kimberlee's advice and slow down with Jared. Speaking of Kimberlee, I hadn't heard from her in a while, and oddly enough, I missed those nagging breakfast calls. I made a quick decision to drop by her place for a pop-up visit.

I knocked on the door then placed my finger over the peep-hole. No one came to the door, but I knew someone was in the house because I could hear the television blaring and those mutts barking like they were mad. I stood there for a moment longer and knocked again. I could hear the floor creak with each footstep as she neared the door.   Anxiously waiting, I tapped my foot until I saw a set of eyes peeking through the blinds, which clapped back together, then the door opened slowly. She was happy to see me so she greeted me as if nothing was wrong but she couldn't hide the pain in her eyes. I knew her like a book, and I knew when something was wrong. She grabbed me and hugged me as soon as I walked through the door. The hug insured me there was a problem. Although I hadn't seen Kimberlee in weeks, I wasn't sure why that warranted a hug. She held on to me as if I would disappear if she let go. In an attempt to mask the pain, she asked about Jared. It didn't work- I could still see it in her eyes.

"What's wrong, cousin? You look awful." I said with brutal honesty.

"It's nothing," she lied.

I looked straight through her, giving her a look that was like a truth serum. When we were younger, that look always pulled the truth out of her. Even when she tried to lie, she would stammer. I kept staring at her hoping she would talk to me. We both stayed in intense silence until she broke down in tears. She walked into the kitchen, grabbed two glasses and a bottle of wine, came back into the room and handed one of them to me before she sat down. She didn't say anything and neither did I. The tension was so thick, you could cut it with a knife. I got up to leave as soon as I finished my first glass of wine.

"Please don't go," she grabbed my arm. "I just need you here with me. Your presence is enough."

Kimberlee didn't say much more but I stayed because she seemed desperate for me to. We sat there in uncomfortable silence for more than two hours: no music, no TV, nothing but the eerie quiet of her living room and a bottle of Riesling. Finally, she broke down and told me that she suspected her husband of cheating. I couldn't believe my ears. Mrs. Perfect had an issue; her prominent doctor husband was allegedly cheating with the maid. She asked me not to tell anyone because she was embarrassed. And though she planned to confront him as soon as he came home, she hadn't mentioned it yet. I didn't plan to tell anybody. To be perfectly honest, Kimberlee was overreacting. She was making an assumption based on information she'd seen on Facebook. I warned Kimberlee about Facebook before she set up the account. I knew from experience the site was nothing but trouble. Countless relationships gave up the ghost because of it.

I watched Kimberlee cry because I didn't know what else to do. She was convinced Eddie Lee was sleeping with the maid. As bad as I wanted it to be a lie, I started to believe he was cheating on her but I didn't speak or move. This was Kimberlee's decision. I wanted to tell her to pack up and leave but I refrained from saying anything. I knew if she left because I said it, she would resent me the moment she got lonely. I was going home to Jared so all of the nights she would spend alone, I would be with someone. Eventually loneliness would consume her and she'd hate me for that advice.

I stayed until she stopped crying. I watched her pack a bag. Finally, she smiled and so did I. I left knowing she'd made her own decision. Somehow she was comforted by my silence. Once Kimberlee left, I knew she would need me and I would be there. I decided to give her a few days alone before I checked back. I had my own man problems to deal with. Something fishy was happening with Jared but I resolved to deal with it until whatever it was reared its head. I'd just be happy and live in the moment. Shonda, a friend of mine from work called as I pulled out of Kimberlee's driveway onto the street.

"What's up girl?'

"Not a whole lot, just leaving Kimberlee's house. What's going on with you?" I asked.

"I just wanted to see if you ladies wanted to meet for drinks at Mary Love's tonight."

I didn't want to turn her down but I wanted to get some quality time in with Jared.

"I'll take a rain check tonight honey. I'm beat, and Kimberlee won't be there. She's not feeling well," I lied.

Shonda groaned, probably rubbing her temples, which was an unconscious habit when she was mad. She didn't express any concern for Kimberlee's well-being. She mumbled something under her breath and the phone went dead. I knew then she was mad, but I didn't care. I wasn't in the mood for Mary Love's, no matter who asked.

My cell rang again. Caller ID told me it was Tomeka. I didn't want to talk so I sent her to the voicemail. Less than five minutes later, the annoying sound of ringing intruded on my quiet time in the car. This time it was Mrs. Young. I gave her the same treatment as Tomeka: voicemail. Mrs. Young could leave a message and I would call her back.

I stopped by The Coffee Shoppe for a hot, Milky Way mocha. I pulled out my laptop and utilized the free Wi-Fi that was available. I needed to get some work done, but I didn't want to be cooped up in the office on such a lovely day. A few hours later, I was still there, working like crazy. I would have never looked up from the monitor if it wasn't for the loud, rumbling noise. My stomach was growling. I ordered a sandwich and a second mocha and continued working. The familiar laughter of a couple in love--, or lust, whatever the case—shifted my attention to my relationship with Jared. I hadn't talked to him all day so I stopped looking for the two-bedroom, one bath condo with all of the amenities, in the perfect location that my client so desperately wanted; picked up my cellie, and called my guy.

"Hey, baby!" He sounded like he was in a good mood.

"Hey, sweetie. What's up? Haven't heard from you today," I said, trying to make a point, without nagging.

"It's been a hectic day. I'm fresh out of class, where are you?"

"Sitting in The Coffee Shoppe, working and waiting for the sandwich I ordered."

Jared asked which location I was at as he invited himself to join me. He said he was less than a block away.

"Order my favorite sandwich and I'll be there in a sec." I could hear the sound of Future's latest album playing in the background before he hung up.

An hour later Jared and I were leaving the spot in separate cars, headed down the interstate in the same direction. By nine o'clock we were creating a love song with the creaking of the springs in my mattress. Jared kissed me the moment we entered the house. It was a kiss like never before, full of fire and ice; hot and cold at the same time. He almost made me come with the mere touch of his lips to mine. I wasn't sure how we'd gone from him not pleasing me to me not being able to control myself when I was near him, but I couldn't remember the last time I'd had a date with my index and middle fingers.

Round one was a quickie. We were both anxious to get to that tingling feeling. Round two, he began at my nipples. His fingers caressed them, then his tongue. He picked me up and carried me to my bedroom. He didn't notice that he almost dropped me before we reached my satin-covered, queen-sized bed. I chuckled a little before the passion in his eyes shut me up. Jared mounted me and took me to Heaven, rocking to the rhythm created by that squeaking bed.

"Oh, baby…I'm…I'm coming. Oh, don't stop," I screamed as I created Grand Canyon size ridges in his back with my nails.

"Who's the man?" he said panting with confidence.

"You are!"

"Who's the man?" he repeated.

I couldn't answer. The air was being sucked from my body with every thrust. The fire was smothering me.

"Who's the man?"

"You are," I whispered.

"Say my name."

"Oh, Omar!"

Everything went cold. He stopped mid-stroke. "Who the hell did you just call me?"

He'd put his pants on before I could respond. The fire that had fueled our lovemaking was now in his eyes. I lay in bed bewildered. I didn't know what had happened.

"You called me Omar! So is that who you think about when you're with me?"

I was awestruck.

"Answer me! Is it?"

The ticking of my wall clock was the only sound. Tick. Tock. It was the reminder of time and chance. I couldn't respond. There was nothing to say.

Jared left. I didn't chase him. I wanted to go after him but there was no need to because I had no explanation for what I'd done. If the roles were reversed, he'd never hear from me again. I had messed up. The front door slammed, but I didn't move.

I lay in bed watching the red blinking light on the digital clock that had never been set. It repeatedly flashed 12:00. The wall clock read 3:00 AM. I was still laying there listening to that lonely tick. My heart beat in unison. With each tick, there was only time and chance. Eventually, my thoughts became a nightmare when I drifted off to sleep.

Knock. Knock. Knock. I awakened to someone beating on my door. I was reluctant to move because I knew it was Jared. I was sure he'd return to get his things, but I didn't want it to end this way. I had no intention of opening the door until he'd had time to calm down. If I let him take his stuff tonight, I'd never talk to him again.

I lay there waiting for him to leave but the knocking only got harder. It sounded like he was trying to kick the door down. I stumbled out of bed, still completely naked and looked out of the peephole. What the hell? It wasn't Jared. It was Omar and he was with Mrs. Young. I couldn't imagine what the two of them could want at this hour, nor did I understand why they would be together. Utter shock made me open the door without going back to get my robe.

"Omar. Mrs. Young." I didn't know what else to say.

They both walked inside without an invitation. Omar closed the door.

"Come on in," I said sarcastically, as I stood fully exposed.

Mrs. Young laughed like a witch. Omar looked me square in the eyes, before he opened his jacket, removed his stainless-steel .40 caliber pistol and placed it on my temple. Mrs. Young cackled again. Omar pulled the trigger.

I jumped up, screamed, and bolted from the bed, leaving an Alicia shaped sweat stain on my sheets. Looking around the room, I realized I was alone. Nobody but me, no sound except for the ticking of the clock. It was six in the morning, time for me to get dressed for work.

By afternoon, I hadn't done anything productive. My mind was on Jared. I knew I'd screwed up. He was a prisoner of my thoughts and so was I. I wanted to call him to explain, but there was nothing to say. I dialed his number, then hung up. I couldn't bring myself to face the rejection. I left for home because I wasn't getting anything accomplished.

The liquor store screamed my name as I passed, so I stopped to get a bottle of wine before I made it home.

"Hi, Alicia." The clerk knew me by name.

"Hey, Brad. Give me the usual." I forced a smile.

He pulled a bottle of Riesling from behind the counter, put it in a brown paper bag, and handed it to me. I gave him thirty-dollars and left the store, not waiting for my change.

Alicia

I hadn't talked to Jared in several weeks. I began to accept the fact that we were over. I'd packed his things and put them in the hall closet. It wasn't much, but if he ever decided he wanted them, they would be ready. It was time for me to find his replacement. My Dear used to say, the best way to get over one man is to get another one. I could hear Mary Love's calling my name.

I roll-called the crew to meet me. As usual, they were down.

A simple, yet sexy outfit was my bait. I paired my favorite red blouse with denim skinny jeans, red pumps, and a small red Coach purse to accentuate. I knew I would be turning heads. I arrived at Mary Love's an hour before the girls so I was tipsy by the time they made it. I needed to be buzzed because I'd decided not to share my anguish with them just yet. The only way I could keep it in was to mask the pain with some happy juice. Tomeka immediately asked about my latest escapade between the sheets with Jared. I told her all of the passionate details about our last roll in the hay. Of course, I purposely left out the part about him leaving me alone in the middle of the night because I'd called him Omar. Once I finished, I told her she needed to buy her a battery-powered boyfriend and give him a name. In my opinion, she was into my personal business way more than she needed to be, which told me she needed a sex life of her own.

Kimberlee didn't drink or talk much, which was very unusual. I knew she was hurting on the inside because normally, we had to beg her to stop bumping her gums about that doctor husband of hers. Everything was Big Doc this, Big Doc that. Now she's sitting with the hush mouth. I told her about that damn Facebook; it's nothing but trouble. I wish I could help her, but what could I say? I'm the same woman who had just lost the love of my life because I called him by the name of the hate of my life, during the best sex of my life. I was a fool, with no advice to share. I almost sat in Mary Love's and got depressed beside Kimberlee. Thinking about what my cousin was going through had me feeling sorry for myself all over again. Then I remembered I was out looking for my replacement, and I couldn't do that sitting down. I heard an old favorite of mine by Destiny's Child start to play so I downed the rest of my wine and bopped my way through the crowd onto the dance floor. With my hands swinging side to side, I danced and sang to the top of my lungs.

It was like no one was in the club with me. The wine had taken me to another place. I rocked and rocked with the ladies from Destiny's Child. When the song ended I headed back toward the table where Tomeka was sitting. She handed me her paper napkin and told me to wipe the sweat from my brow, then asked me if I would be okay at Mary Love's alone. I didn't want Tomeka to leave, but I knew she wasn't enjoying herself. Since her lifestyle change, she didn't dance, drink, or do any of the sinful things that happened in bars. I knew she'd only come because it was our friend ritual. Besides, Kimberlee had already bailed on us. I told Tomeka to go ahead, assuring her I would be fine. I watched her walk away, then stopped the waitress to bring me more wine. That song had me thinking aloud, "Damn, I need a soldier."

"Be careful what you ask for. Are you sure you can handle a soldier?"

I looked up and there he stood: Mr. Tall, Dark, and Handsome, the man of my dreams, and definitely a soldier.
I shrieked before I stormed away to the ladies' room. I pushed my way into the restroom and let the door slam behind me, screaming like Florida Evans from *Good Times*. "Damn! Damn! Damn!"

A short, light skinned, yet unattractive chick with a front row full of gold teeth and an orange weave that screamed ghetto approached me and asked if I was okay. I told her I was fine. I just needed a minute. At that moment I wished I had magical powers because I wanted to make myself invisible and exit the club without having to deal with Omar.

When I got home, I couldn't get Omar's image out of my head. I knew eventually I would have to deal with him again, but I wasn't prepared to do it at Mary Love's. Over and over, I saw those same baggy jeans, that LRG shirt, and those Air Force One sneakers. I was lucky to get out of the club without running back into him. A steady flow of tears covered my face. I was mad at myself because I should have been able to handle him. I should have said everything I'd practiced so many times in the bathroom mirror. I shouldn't have let him get to me that way. I picked myself up from the sofa, dragging to the bar. I had to have a drink, otherwise I wouldn't sleep at all. Three goblets of wine didn't do anything for me as far as making me drowsy. I needed something more, something stronger. I immediately started to think about how good it would feel to get high again. I hadn't smoked in a while, so I knew it wouldn't take much of a joint to get me right. I thought about the last time I'd smoked and remembered I'd stashed some away for a time like this. I ran to the closet in my bedroom, grabbed a foot stool, and pulled down the Nike shoe box that was filled with memories. There were pictures from high school, old love letters, and last but not least, that dime sack of weed I was searching for. I rolled a funny cigarette with joint papers that were also in the box. One long, hard drag had me feeling the effects of the drug. My mind started racing. I knew from the first hit I wouldn't be able to stop. I knew I'd picked up a new, bad habit. Damn, Omar. He was the reason I started smoking, stopped, then started all over again.

It seemed like everything I did these days reminded me of Omar, especially since Jared left. The euphoria from the joint took me back in time to my date with Omar. I closed my eyes, reminiscing about the good ole days.

After the bowling alley, two glasses of wine, and Omar pouring his heart out to me, I was smitten. His presence alone had me horny. I went back and forth with myself about not giving it up on the first date. I'd never had a one-night stand, and didn't have any intentions on doing so. A brother had to put in some work to get his hands in my pot of honey. Omar was different though. He was very charming. There was something about him that made everyone like him. I'm telling you the man could sell sand in a desert. He gazed into my eyes as he finished sharing the intimate details of his aspirations with me. I diverted my eyes to the floor. It made me nervous to look at him like that. He held my hand, and asked me to tell him something about me. I'd never been good at the job interview style "tell me about yourself" conversation, and I told him so.

"Mind if I smoke?"

I told him it was okay before I knew what he was talking about. I watched Omar take a cigar from the bag the wine was in. I didn't smoke, so there were no ashtrays in the house. I walked to the kitchen to get a small ceramic bowl he could use as a makeshift ashtray. When I returned, he was removing the tobacco from the cigar.

"What the hell are you doing?" I asked as I watched him refill the cigar with reefer. "Ain't no illegal activity going down in here!"

Omar kept licking and tucking the cigar.

"Did you hear me?" I asked.

"Yep, I heard you. But this ain't illegal, at least not everywhere. It goes down in Cali and Colorado! Besides, I know you smoke, girl. Don't try to tell me that you've never had a blunt. Just calm down, it's relaxing. You'll love it." He looked at me through those big, beautiful eyes.

I melted. "No I've never smoked anything, not even a cigarette."

"You should try this."

"No, thank you. I'll leave the smoking to you. Go ahead and smoke, but don't leave no traces of that up in here."

He chuckled a bit, inhaled, then blew the smoke in my face, staring seductively at me.

"What?" That was the best response I could muster up. I was in awe. I don't know how or why, but the way he smoked turned me on. It looked sexy on him.

"Seriously, Alicia, you're telling me you've never tried this?"

"Never." I'd been reduced to one word answers.

"So that means you've never had sex while you were high."

"Nope." He was getting to me.

"You should try it sometime; it'll take you to unimaginable heights."

"Okay, just one puff." It was far too easy for him to wear me down.

Before I knew it, we had smoked an entire blunt, and he was in my bed. Omar was absolutely right, no one had ever made me feel the way he did that night.

I had to shake those thoughts. I couldn't stand to think about Omar and the memories I shared with him. With tears in my eyes, I picked the contents of the shoe box up from the floor and put it back in the closet. Thoughts about Omar led to thoughts about Jared. I finished my joint and passed out cold.

Tomeka

Over and over, I saw Malik packing his bags while Khalil and Khalik held on to his legs. I knew Malik would have left if the boys hadn't walked in when they did. Who did Malik think he was? I didn't deserve the way I was being treated and I wasn't going to take it anymore.

After I took the boys to daycare, I cooked a one-person breakfast. Malik loves bacon so I fried a few extra slices for him to make a bacon sandwich, whenever he finally pulled himself out of bed. I didn't want to cook for him, but I didn't feel like hearing his mouth either. I was determined it would be a peaceful day. Arguing all the time was getting old, and I wasn't going to let six slices of bacon ruin the day.

I took my breakfast into the bedroom so I could eat while I watched TV. I hoped Malik wouldn't bother me. He'd slept in the guest room and I hadn't missed him at all; it was the best sleep I'd had in ages.

Around ten o'clock, I could hear Malik moving around in the hall bathroom. He was so predictable. All I had to do was wait. I knew he'd eat his breakfast, shower, then leave until the wee hours of the morning. Normally that bothered me, but not today. I was on pins and needles waiting for him to leave.

Like clockwork, Malik was pulling his Cadillac Escalade out of the driveway by noon. At 12:01, I was packing his bags.

I'd warned Malik about this day. It was obvious he didn't believe fat meat was greasy. He didn't believe I had it in me to leave, or in this case, put him out.

I started in our bedroom by rummaging around the same drawers he'd gone through when he tried to walk out on me. All of his boxers, briefs, basketball shorts, socks, and T-shirts were slung into a duffel bag. Next, I took cologne, watches, rings, and any other bling and threw them in a cash lock box. I didn't plan to leave any stone unturned. Malik was raising up out of my crib today. I went to our walk-in closet, a closet big enough to fit two full size beds, looked around and smiled at Malik's prized possession- his collection of Air Jordan's. He had every pair in every color combination. Malik was the kind of guy who loved "things" so much he always had a way to get money. He's the man who will hustle until he's filthy rich, just for sneakers, cars, and clothes. I wanted to take everything outside to start a bonfire but I wasn't waiting to exhale, just yet. I exercised restraint. It would be enough for me to see the look on his face when he realized I was putting him out of a house he was paying for.

The thought of losing my man sent the troops. Tears marched down my face like an army of men at war. I didn't want to put Malik out. I simply wanted him to realize there's more to life than money. I wanted him to stop neglecting me and the boys. I need more from Malik than the cars and clothes. He thinks loving us means lavishing us with gifts, but that's not love. I need him to be here.

I went back to the bathroom medicine cabinet, taking the last of my stash and fired up. I wasn't worried about being caught. Malik wouldn't be home for hours. The weed had me thinking again: *It's time to get yourself together. You don't need Malik. You can make it on your own.*

I was motivated to get up and pack the rest of his stuff. I wasn't sure how I would drop the bomb on the boys, but where there's a will, there's a way and I would think of something.

I called my mom to see if she would get the twins from school. Of course, she was happy to oblige. She never passed up an opportunity to see her only grandchildren, not to mention my dad would lose his mind if he didn't see them several days out the week.

I went through the house like a Tasmanian Devil, packing and cleaning as I went. When I say I packed up everything, I mean, I packed up everything that belonged to Malik and neatly arranged it in the garage. Family pictures had been replaced with photos of Khalil and Khalik. My home was in perfect order and I was ready to get on with my life. I was tired of asking Malik to change.

Instead, it was time for me to change. First order of business: get rid of Malik. Check.

I finished packing pretty late in the evening. Alicia called to see if I would meet her at Mary Love's. In most instances, I didn't like being there. But tonight, I need some release so once again I agreed to go. I met up with the usual crew, and we cut up for a while. I noticed something was going on with both Alicia and Kimberlee. Kimberlee was obviously sullen, but Alicia tried to hide what was going on. She drank and danced the night away, but I knew my friend well. She couldn't hide it from me. I chose not to pry; they would tell me in due time. Besides, I wouldn't have been a good listener. My mind was on Malik. I wanted to be home when he came in so I ditched Alicia right after Kimberlee left.

By 2:30 A.M., the roaring of the garage startled me out of my sleep. Even after hanging out with the girls, I'd managed to make it home before Malik did. I'd fallen asleep on the sofa waiting for him. I knew he'd noticed the boxes because he didn't come into the house right away. My stomach was doing cartwheels. An uneasy feeling swept over me. I could sense him looking through the bags and boxes.

The door slammed.

"Meka!" He called out in a panic.

"What's up?" I asked nonchalantly.

"You tell me."

I knew exactly where this was going; he was in shock.

"Oh, you mean the boxes in the garage?" I tried not to smirk as I talked. "That's your stuff."

"I know that much, smart ass. Why is my stuff in the garage?" he asked, huffing.

"You're moving out. You can do it now or in the morning, I don't care when. I've saved you the trouble of packing your things. All you have to do is remove them from my house within the next twenty-four hours. Goodnight," I said holding back the tears. I didn't want Malik to see me cry, I had to face this head on, like a woman.

"Your house?" He asked, defensively.

"My house." I held my ground.

"This is my house, and I'm not going anywhere." He was fuming.

I walked over to him, giving him the title work.

"My house," I said, turning to walk out on him. "Malik, this house belongs to me, sweetie. Read the paperwork."

I didn't have to look back to know his mouth had dropped to the floor. It had just hit him that he'd put it in my name. Yes. This was MY house. I added a twist to my hips, simply for his sake. Eventually he would see, you don't miss your water 'til the well runs dry and his well was tapped.

I took pleasure in what I'd done. As far as I was concerned, the relationship was over and the monkey was off my back. Malik, however, had other plans. He ran up behind me, grabbing my elbow.

"Don't do this Tomeka. It will hurt the boys." He couldn't look at me when he spoke.

"I get it. You care about the boys today. Really, Malik? Really? Don't touch me, I'm done. The boys will get over it. I don't want to talk about it. Goodnight." I snatched my arm from his grasp, continuing to the bedroom. I was serious about being done. I pulled the comforter back, and slid underneath. The coolness of the sheets hit my bare feet, I closed my eyes, sealing the deal. Malik moved toward his side of the bed. Funny how he suddenly wanted to be near me; Malik had slept in the guest bedroom since our last fight.

"Can I lay with you?"

I felt a tingle in my triangle. I wanted him to lay with me. Being real with myself, I loved Malik, but I had to be strong.

"Would you listen if I told you no?" I asked, ignoring the tingle.

"Probably not," he chuckled.

I didn't answer or laugh. I couldn't make it easy for Malik. That was the problem; things always went his way. He stripped down to his boxers before snuggling up against me. I looked at him and rolled my eyes. He was getting to me but I had to keep up the façade.

"Meka."

"What?"

"We need to talk." He barely spoke above a whisper.

"What's to talk about?" Malik was annoying me. It was amazing to me how the tables were turning. "Not now Malik, it's late, I'm sleepy. What's done is done, let's leave it alone." I rolled over, turning my back to him.

"We need to talk tonight. You want me to leave in the morning, right?"

"Right." His question warranted only a one-word answer.

"Well, can you give me a chance to talk to you before I go?"

I wanted to treat Malik the way he'd treated me so many nights. Something inside me told me to scream to the top of my lungs telling him there was nothing to talk about. I wanted to tell him I had made up my mind and I wanted him out of my life. It was best for me to move on, but instead of using my head, I used my heart.

"Talk," I said without enthusiasm.

Before he spoke a word, he patted his chest for me to rest my head there. Reluctantly, I moved closer to him, but I didn't lay my head down. Malik was trying to reel me in and he almost had me, hook, line, and sinker.

"I'm tired. Get to it, will you?" I said with a yawn.

Malik pulled me onto him, wrapping his arms around me. "I know I messed up Meka, but I can't live without you and my sons. Give me a chance to get settled. I want to be secure financially so I can take care of yall like I want to, and I promise I will leave the game. We'll get married. I'll even go to college."

He seemed sincere. It felt good to hear him talk about marrying me, but I couldn't allow myself to fall for the "okie-doke". I knew the game. He'd act like a man long enough to reel me in. Then he'd throw me back out to swim with the sharks. Malik had done this to me one too many times. Things had been too easy for him. An inner strength possessed me like a demon. I'm sure my eyes rolled back in my head and my body shook.

"Stop it Malik. I don't want to hear your lies." I paused for added effect. "Leave by morning."

I wiggled out of his arms, turning my back to him.

Malik was quiet.

I was scared.

Malik was never short of words. This was serious. I cracked one eye opened, looking out the side of it. He was staring at me.

"What is it, Malik?"

He got up, put his clothes on and left.

Tomeka

I wondered if I was an alcoholic, or a weed head. I knew I was one of them, but I couldn't figure out which. Lately, every time there was a problem, I turned to a joint or a drink. That couldn't be good for me. I wanted to stop drinking and smoking…just not tonight.

I wasn't sure if I was ready for a life without Malik. When he walked out, my world was instantly in shambles. Couldn't live with him. Couldn't live without him.

Through agony, I allowed him to walk out on me. My heart begged him to turn around. Reality let him go. It was over for Malik and me. This was the best move for us.

More tears.

I was crying again because of Malik. Love shouldn't hurt like this. With each tear came a thought. Why didn't I have a man like Eddie Lee?

I picked up my cell, let my thumb rest on the numbers, then put it down. Who was I kidding? There was absolutely no one for me to call at this time of morning. Everyone was asleep like I should have been. Everyone, except possibly Eddie Lee. I needed someone to lean on. Again, I picked up the phone, but put it down.

Gumption came from deep within. Or maybe it was the six pack of beer I'd inhaled in less than an hour.

"Eddie Lee"

"Tomeka?"

"Yes. How are you?"

"Not so good, Doc. I could use some company."

I sighed and crushed my joint in the ash tray as I waited for his response. He didn't respond right away so I wanted to take the words back. Too bad. That's the thing about words, once they are out there, there's no getting them back.

His silence hit me in the stomach like a sledge hammer. It also infuriated me. For the life of me I didn't understand why he'd offered me his number if he didn't want me to use it.

"Eddie Lee?"

"I'm still here."

"Will you come?"

"What about Malik?" He asked.

"What about Kimberlee?" I countered.

"Kimberlee's fine. I left a few hours ago to deliver a baby. She's probably sound asleep because she is used to me keeping late hours. Now, what about Malik?"

"He's gone. I need you."

"On the way."

I couldn't believe it'd been so simple.

It took longer than I expected for Eddie Lee to arrive. I wanted to call him because I was getting impatient, but I waited. Finally, my dogs began barking uncontrollably. That told me someone was outside the house. I ran to the front door to let the doctor in. I didn't want him to knock on the door because of the possibility that it would wake Khalil and Khalik.

Sheer disappointment covered my face. It was Malik.

I stood in the doorway. My heart was at my feet. Malik walked past me as I stood holding the door. I didn't move.

He looked back at me.

"What's wrong with you? Close the door, and close your mouth."

Malik hadn't been back five minutes, and we were already playing Malik says again and it irked me bad.

I folded my arms across my chest.

"What are you doing here, Malik?"

"I live here Tomeka and I'm not leaving. I thought about playing your little game but I refuse to be made a fool of. I'm staying in the house that I'm paying for, and we're going to work this thing out."

My phone rang before Malik could finish his speech. His eyes darted to the wall clock.

4:30am.

My eyes darted to my caller id.

Eddie Lee.

I answered without hesitation.

"Alicia?"

"Huh? This is Eddie Lee." He said bewildered.

I didn't stop the facade.

"Yeah, Alicia. Malik's back home. Call me tomorrow."

The call disconnected.

I looked up at Malik who'd been staring down my throat the whole time. My heart pounded. I was nervous as hell.

He grabbed my hand.

"Let's go to bed, you've got to be up in about an hour."

Like a robot, I did as I was told because Malik said.

Alicia

I was sitting on my bed, finishing another glass of wine, feeling like the pitiful reality to Kimberlee's prediction about me and Jared. He hadn't called in weeks, and I'd resisted the urge to call him, although I held on to the hope that he'd call me so he could get his stuff. Deep down, I wanted him to call so I could apologize. Actually, I needed him to call. I took a long sip of wine, picking up my cell phone. I dialed the first few digits of his number, then hung up. I bit my bottom lip, staring at the LCD screen of my mobile phone. I tried to decide if my heart could bear the rejection I was sure I would face. I put the phone down, but picked up a joint from my nightstand.

Two or three hits of weed would give me the "don't care" attitude I needed to endure the call to Jared. One more pull and I called, only this time I dialed *67 to block my number.

"Hello." He answered on the second ring.

"Jared," I barely spoke above a whisper.

"Helloooooo."

I cleared my throat, and spoke again before he could hang up. "Um, Jared. It's Alicia."

Silence.

"Jared, are you there?" I almost hung up. My pride was bruised.

"Are you sure you dialed the right number. This isn't Omar."

I sensed the sarcasm in his tone. Again, I almost disconnected the phone.

The marijuana kicked in, giving me a false sense of security. "I know who I called. I want to talk to you, Jared."

"I'm listening." It wasn't the response I wanted but it sure wasn't the reaction I expected.

"I'm sorry, Jared. I wish I could explain what happened, but I can't. All I can do is apologize."

The ticking of my bedroom clock, reminded me of time and chance. I refused to give up. I wanted to smooth things over but I could only do that if somehow Jared would agree to a visit.

He was unresponsive so I talked on, "I understand you must really hate me, Jared. I feel awful. I have kicked myself a thousand times. At this point, I can't do anything more than apologize, whether you accept or not is totally on you. Meanwhile, I've packed the things you left here. I'd appreciate it if you would stop by to pick them up. I need closure, and I can't get that if your things are cluttering my space." I laughed at myself as I tried the ole "transfer of emotions trick" I'd seen on the classic hit, *Two Can Play That Game.*

"I'll be by in an hour or so."

I wasn't exactly sure what he was feeling, but I was very excited I'd gotten him to agree to come over. As far as I was concerned, the phone call was a success.

Jared sat in the car for ten minutes before making his way to my front door. I knew because I watched him from my living room window. When he opened his car door to exit, I snapped the blinds closed then started spraying rain shower scented air freshener all over the room. I didn't want Jared to get a whiff of the strong aroma that was lingering in the air from my smoking habit.

I was bowled over when I opened the door. Jared's attire was different than usual. His Akoo jeans hung dangerously low, and he was also sporting a matching Akoo hoodie that screamed thug. However, I was surprised more by the fact that his locs were neatly twisted. I wondered who he found to do his hair because over the entire course of our relationship, he always acted like I was the only loc stylist in town. It was always a matter of life or death when it came to me maintaining his hair. I must admit, his hair looked good, but not better than the job I would've done. It felt like a violation for someone else's hands to do the work I'd done so long. It was like someone had splashed red paint across a masterpiece that had been perfectly crafted by these hands. I made my assessment of him within a matter of seconds.

I motioned for him to come inside, still unsure of what I would say. He entered without hesitation. Maybe he wasn't as upset as I thought. I offered Jared a glass of wine. He refused, telling me he'd only stopped by to get his things. Not only did he look different but his persona was not the same. I handed him the two Target bags filled with his stuff. He turned abruptly toward the door to leave. My heart dropped to my feet, my world stood still. Time and chance. Time and chance. With every tick of the clock, I was missing an opportunity. If I didn't make a move soon, I would lose Jared indefinitely.

Jared walked out of my apartment and closed the door behind him. I wanted to call out to him but I couldn't find the courage. I allowed him to leave. I didn't deserve him. I peeped out the window, watching him follow the sidewalk to his car. The bottom line was I'd messed up and there was no turning back. I had to move on. I dragged myself to the bedroom, back to the glass of wine. Back to the weed. Back to the ticking of the clock. I had let my chance slip away. It was time to move forward. I hit the joint and leaned back against the headboard.

Pure frustration sent me to the bathroom for a long, steamy, hot bath. I turned the hot water on full blast, poured in some bubble bath, then returned to my room to get my bottle, ashtray, and *He Never Said Sorry*, the book I was reading by Ashley Cruse. Before I could remove my clothes, I thought I heard knocking. I didn't feel like being bothered. All I wanted to do was clear my head, but somebody was intruding.

I looked out the peephole; Jared came back. I tied the belt on my robe and opened the door.

"I thought you wanted to talk. Ain't you gonna invite me in?"

I opened the door wider, did a sweeping motion with my hand. Once he was inside, for lack of something better to say, I commented on the way he looked.

"What do you mean, I look different?" he asked.

"Well, your clothes. You normally don't dress so thuggish." I looked down at the floor, tugging the belt on my robe.

"Oh, this." He laughed. "I did this for you. Figured since you started calling me Omar, the least I could do was look like him for you. What do you think?"

"I think I don't want to do this, Jared. Did you come back to argue?"

He laughed again. Frankly, I didn't see the humor in it so I was a bit irritated.

"I came back to talk but I can leave if I caught you at a bad time. I see you're in a robe and the place reeks of weed. Do you have company?"

"I don't have company. We can talk," I answered.

"Are you smoking weed now? That is so unattractive and unbecoming for a woman of your caliber. I thought you were more than your average hood chick, but I guess drug use is another one of those Omar hang-ups, huh? What is it about that brother you can't let go of? I've listened to you constantly bash him; now you represent everything he is. First you're calling me his name in the middle of our session. Next you're smoking again. It sickens me. I came back to talk to you because you're killing me softly. The feelings I have for you are slowly dying. It's almost like I don't know you anymore."

I couldn't speak because I didn't know what to say. I didn't find the words until Jared turned to leave after a few minutes of intense silence. I'd been staring at the floor the entire time he was talking.

"Please don't go, Jared. I need you." I talked fast out of desperation. I had to get his attention. It was now or never. "I need you. If I didn't realize it before, I realize it now. This time apart has been hell on me. I can't go on like this." Tears streamed down my face. If all he needed was confirmation I didn't want Omar, I could manage that. Once I started to treat Jared the way he'd always treated me then our relationship would be solid.

To my surprise, Jared hugged me. He hated to see me cry. He reminded me the situation was far from over, but he told me we could work on repairing our relationship. No sooner than the words left his mouth, Jared was all over me, removing my robe.

The buzzing of my cell interrupted what we had going on. Jared motioned for me to answer. I didn't want to ruin the moment so I shook my head no. The timing couldn't have been worse, not to mention the caller was relentless. They called repeatedly.

"Do something with your phone, Alicia." Jared was irritated.

I was disappointed to see that whoever was calling me had blocked their number. If the caller had tried an hour earlier, I would've answered because of the possibility of it being Jared. However, with Jared by my side, no one else stood a chance. I told Jared it was a client, and silenced my phone.

Tomeka

The annoying sound of buzzing from my alarm clock started my morning promptly at 6:00 AM. I hit the snooze button and rolled over in bed. I needed a few extra minutes every morning to get myself in the mood to get up and move around. The twins were enrolled in a daycare that ran like a school. The program was set up to prepare preschoolers for the onset of elementary school so the boys couldn't be late. It was no secret that I wasn't a morning person but I had to get up and make things happen.

Malik, on the other hand, went to bed late and woke up early. Every morning he was up at the crack of dawn, taking care of his dogs. It pissed me off that he could get up before six to water and feed his mutts, but he wouldn't take the boys to school. Living with Malik was like being a single mother.

The alarm sounded a second time fifteen minutes later. I knew for a fact I couldn't sleep any longer without making Khalil and Khalik tardy to school. Trust me, I'd tried it before. I sat up slowly, placing both feet on the floor, sleepily rubbing my eyes. I could hear the water running in the bathroom, so I knew Malik was in there. For a split second I thought about asking him to dress the boys and take them to school. That thought disappeared faster than chicken at a black family reunion because I didn't feel like arguing. It was a frustrating, pointless battle so I spared myself the irritation.

I prodded myself to get moving just as Malik exited the bathroom, whistling. I frowned at his joy. In my mind, there was absolutely nothing to whistle about so early in the morning. I stood from the bed, stretching before I could walk. Malik walked over to me, wrapping his arms around my waist.

"Good morning, baby," he said cheerfully.

"What's so good about it?" I asked sarcastically.

I still wasn't feeling Malik. I wanted to work things out with him, but I didn't want to make it easy. After all, Malik was always full of empty promises. His promises from the night before didn't mean anything to me; he'd have to show me that he was sincere. I was tired of falling for his lies.

"Everything about this morning is good, baby. For starters, we are here together, alive and well." He gently touched my chin, pulling my mouth to his for a kiss.

"Malik, please. We are here together every morning, alive and well. What's special about today?"

I walked away from him toward the bathroom, not giving him a chance to respond. My toothbrush was calling my name.

"Well, why don't you rest a while longer and let me take care of the boys."

My eyes lit up. I couldn't believe my ears. "Are you serious, honey? You're taking the boys to school?"

"Correction. I'm getting the boys dressed AND taking them to school today. You're sleeping in."

Malik didn't have to tell me twice. I crawled back into bed immediately before he could change his mind.

Ironically enough, I wasn't sleepy once Malik left with my babies but I stayed in bed anyway, determined to rest. I used the remote control to flip through the channels. The news, sports highlights, cooking shows, and infomercials controlled the air waves. There wasn't much to choose from so early in the morning so I gave up. I closed my eyes once again, trying to find sleep but gave up on that as well; it just wasn't happening.

As I lay there with closed eyes, I thought about Tyler. He was an extraordinary young man and I didn't understand how something so tragic happened to him. It didn't seem fair to me.

When Malik arrived home, I was dressed and ready to leave. I couldn't shake my thoughts of Tyler so I decided to visit him.

"Where are you going?" Malik asked the moment he saw me.

"To the hospital to visit Tyler."

Malik didn't have to speak for me to notice his annoyance. His expression told it all.

"But I bought breakfast. I figured we'd eat, then lie in bed and watch TV until we pass out again. The boys are gone and the house is quiet. You're always complaining about not getting to sleep in and now that I've given you a chance you're leaving. So I guess your date with Tyler can't wait until later?"

His eyes pleaded with me not to leave. I felt guilty enough to stay before realizing that Malik was feeling the same emotions I'd felt so many times. He didn't care then, therefore I didn't care now.

"Don't get soft on me Malik. It's not a date; Tyler almost died in our driveway and I'm going to support him until he recovers. If you ask me, you should do the same."

"Screw Tyler! As far as I'm concerned, he should have died if he lived only to steal my woman. I can't believe you're going to leave me here to have breakfast alone while you gallivant around that hospital with another man."

"How selfish, Malik. I'm going to visit Tyler whether you like it or not. I don't know how to make you understand my feelings toward him and I'm not going to try anymore!"

"Go Tomeka. I'm not mad at you. Contrary to popular belief, I do understand your feelings for Tyler. What I don't understand is how you can complain about taking your children to school because it's too early, but you don't have a problem leaving early to visit Tyler."

Malik had a point, but it didn't matter to me. I left anyway. I had to check on Tyler. A smidgeon of guilt swept over my body, enough to give me a small chill. The drive to the hospital allowed me time to think. I was glad Malik was making an effort but one day of help couldn't take away my previous hurt.

Tyler was a pleasure as usual. I didn't stay very long because he'd started a rehab program and was being wheeled out shortly after I arrived. I told him I'd come later and left the room.

For some reason, I thought of Eddie Lee while I was there, probably because I often saw him on my trips to visit Tyler. I secretly hoped to see him today, if only in passing. I felt bad about calling him to come over, then having to leave him hanging because Malik came home. I wanted to go to the car but my legs took me to the obstetrics wing. Eddie Lee was one of the top obstetricians in the county so he delivered most of the babies in town. I didn't hear any cussing and screaming from women in labor as I walked the halls so I stopped for a moment staring through the window at the babies who were new to this world. I smiled as I thought of the best day of my life, when Khalil and Khalik were born. Turning to walk away, I felt a hand on my shoulder.

"Hello again, Tomeka. How are you?"

I was a tad embarrassed, feeling like Eddie Lee knew I was there looking for him, but I played it off.

"Well, hello there, Mister. I was visiting Tyler but they took him to therapy so I decided to have a look at the babies."

"Aren't they precious? I love children. Maybe one of these days, I'll have a child of my own. Kimberlee promised me we could try, but I know it's not going to happen. She's too selfish."

He looked down after he made his statement. I wasn't sure if he really meant to express that thought aloud.

"Oh, don't tell me about someone being selfish. I'm having a battle of my own in that department."

Eddie Lee didn't respond. We both stood gazing at the babies. I could see the passion in his eyes. He seriously longed to be a dad. I felt sorry for him because I knew Kimberlee was adamant about keeping her figure, but my intuition told me that her husband wouldn't be around long if she didn't get with the program. Simply being in his presence made me want to jump his bones. Kimberlee is my girl though, and I'd never cross that line but that didn't mean the next woman would feel the same.

We stood for what seemed like hours, both in our own worlds, consumed by our thoughts before either of us spoke.

"I'm sorry about last night. I had no idea Malik was coming back." I said in an attempt to apologize.

Eddie Lee shook his head, telling me there was no need for detail. He quickly changed the subject.

"How about a quick breakfast? Hospital food is normally not my idea of good food, but Mrs. Mable is here today and she makes a mean omelet. What do you say?"

I nodded in agreement as Eddie Lee led the way to the cafeteria.

Breakfast had an awkward start to say the least. I didn't like the way Mrs. Mable looked at me when Eddie Lee ordered my omelet.

"I usually don't make this omelet for anyone but the good doctor. It's called the Dr. Washington special and he's the only person who's ever had it."

There was no hint of playfulness in Mrs. Mable's tone. She was serious as a heart attack. I might have been afraid if Eddie Lee hadn't stepped in.

"This will be the only exception, Mrs. Mable," he laughed. "Tomeka's a friend of the family and she's having a rough morning. I thought your cooking would bring her some cheer."

Mrs. Mable seemed flattered and lightened up a bit.

"Well, just this once." She smiled and told us it wouldn't take long to whip them up. Then she pointed to a table and told us to have a seat and she'd bring the omelets out.

My giggle box was in full effect. Not only was Eddie Lee a wonderful man, he had a wonderful sense of humor. I laughed myself right out of my chair onto the floor. Eddie Lee rushed over to help me. As he pulled me up, there was a glimmer in his eyes that made me tingle. I wondered if he wanted me. Eddie Lee had no clue, but I'd have his baby today if he asked me.

"Are you okay?" He asked behind a slight chuckle.

It was apparent he wanted to be sure I was okay before he laughed aloud.

"I'm fine," I answered laughing at myself.

I didn't look at Eddie Lee when I spoke for fear of revealing the feelings that were bopping around in my head. I didn't know where my desires had originated from so suddenly but I had to get away from Eddie Lee, and I had to get away quick! I told Eddie Lee goodbye abruptly, almost running to my car.

Alicia

It was two-thirty in the morning. Jared wasn't home. I'd allowed him to move in with me. Add a tally to my list of mistakes. I started to feel alone in the relationship the moment he moved in. Somehow when the subject came up, I thought it would strengthen our bond. Boy, was I wrong.

By 2:45 I was fuming. This was the third weekend in a row Jared had promised to spend some quality time with me; the third weekend in a row I'd been stood up by my live in boyfriend.

Everything was spiraling out of control. Kimberlee seemed to be avoiding me. I couldn't figure out what was going on with her, and I was worried. Shonda was being weird, and Tomeka was going in a different direction from all of us. She was always at a church function, or somewhere with her new friend, Tina. The biggest weight was Jared. He was no longer in school. He dressed like a thug and kept late hours nearly every day of the week. Jared didn't treat me bad, but I didn't feel like number one in his life. He wasn't the same Alicia radar who had chased me around Target for months. Somehow, I no longer had the upper hand. My gut told me there was another woman. My heart told me the same thing. I knew I needed to pay attention to the signs. Listen carefully. Watch. Whatever is done in the dark will come to light.

I didn't want to look for it because I was actually afraid of what I might find, and I wasn't sure if I could handle the truth.

The truth—the one thing that either hurts or sets you free. I wasn't ready for either. I would not look for it. It would have to slap me in the face. I was tired of crying so I held it in, but I couldn't stop the heavy beating of my heart. My palms were sweaty. Where was Jared? What was he doing and with whom was he doing it? I picked up the phone to call him, but put it down. P-R-I-D-E. That five-letter word stopped me from dialing.

At 2:55, the house phone rang. I debated with myself before answering.

"Hello."

"Hey."

"What are you doing?"

"Nothing, I'm sleep," I lied.

"Get up, I'm on my way home. Take your clothes off. Be naked when I get there. Your man is horny."

I put the phone down, bewildered. Who the hell did Jared think he was? I'd spent the entire evening home alone and he had the nerve to call right before three and ask me to be naked. He was treating me like a late night booty call and I didn't like it. I was on the verge of hating Jared; he'd become Omar right before my eyes.

I turned over, trying to force sleep, but the butterflies in my stomach would not allow it. I'd rather face the demons that haunted my sleep than wait up for Jared with those butterflies. At least with the nightmares, I could save myself by waking up. Reality on the other hand, was a force to be reckoned with all the time. There was no escape.

I fell asleep before I knew it. I fought a battle with that nightmare of Omar and Mrs. Young behind my closed eyelids. But this time when Omar tried to shoot me, I ran like a roadrunner and my son chased me like Wile E. Coyote.

It was 4:15 and Jared was still out. I was pissed. Tears welled in the corners of my eyes, but wouldn't fall. I picked up my cell, stared at it for a while. I didn't call Jared. There was nothing to say. I hated him and I hated being left alone with the ticking of that clock. I didn't want to go back to sleep because I wasn't ready to face Omar either. I lay in bed without blinking or moving, just wondering if the one Jared was with was better than me. I wondered how she looked and moved; how she sounded when she called his name. Jared was cheating on me; that was a no-brainer.

At 4:55, I went to the living room bar and poured a glass of wine, thinking maybe I could drink myself into a coma. I wanted to get so buzzed that nothing would faze me. The wine felt good going down, but it wasn't enough so I did the usual and fired up a joint. I'd rolled the joint for my morning smoke, but I needed it now. Everything slowed down, except my heart and mind.

I heard the jingle of keys in the front door at 5:15. He was coming home almost three hours after he called. My heartbeat was fast and intense like the rotors of a helicopter. I jumped from the sofa, headed for the bedroom. I didn't want Jared to know I'd been waiting up for him or that I'd been on the brink of tears.

"Alicia, baby, are you up?"

Jared pulled the covers back. I lay there motionless. I was heated and wasn't giving him the satisfaction of attention. I didn't give a damn if he knew I was awake. I was going to ignore him. I wanted to make him feel as alone as I had for hours.

"Why aren't you naked? I thought I told you to be naked for me. Take off your clothes."

Jared removed his shoes, sagging jeans, and oversized T-shirt. He undressed down to his boxers, then took them off, and climbed in bed with me.

"Aliciaaaaa," he sang.

I didn't move. He snuggled up against me, putting his naked body against mine. He ran his hand along my backside and worked on removing my pajama bottoms. I was lying on my left side so he was able to get the right side down. He pulled and tugged on the other side, but my pants didn't budge. Jared continued on as if I were inviting. He kissed me overpoweringly on my mouth. I didn't respond. I was tired of being left alone all the time. Every night Jared was out, I sat up, waiting for him to come home. I never asked questions because it upset him when I did.

Jared finally succeeded in getting me naked. He kissed me softly and sensually, starting at my toes. He kissed them one by one, then moved his way up my legs, past my Niagara Falls, then detoured to my belly button. He went up to the twins, giving both of them the same amount of attention with his tongue. I tried to resist but he was hitting my weak spot. I moaned, allowing only a miniature sound to escape my mouth. My lips were pressed together, trying to hold in all of the noise. I didn't want to please Jared, and I didn't want Jared to please me.

"Ummmm," I moaned reluctantly.

Jared was still kissing the twins. His hands moved carefully down my body until they were on the man in the boat rowing his way to Niagara Falls. He dipped his two fingers inside me then put them in his mouth, closed his eyes, and savored the taste of my sweetness like he'd done so many nights before. His fingers returned to that man in the boat, dipped inside of me again. This time he rubbed me there, hitting my spot.

"Ummm," I moaned again, with less resistance.

Jared was winning. His fingers moved about my spot and loved me like I'd loved myself a million times. He made me feel better than I ever did. Jared loved me long and hard that morning. I gave him all of me, loved him long and hard back. At the end of a good ride, I balled my fists and hit him without stopping. I pounded his chest like a mad gorilla. I was angry at him for making me love him. I wanted to make him feel like I felt when he was out. He always got his way with me. I was officially a sucker for love. I needed to snap back to reality.

When we finished I went into the bathroom to clean up. I returned to the room with a towel for him. He was sprawled across the bed, legs open, arms up. I wiped all of the parts of his body he used to love me. I went into the hallway to drop the two towels into the dirty clothes hamper. I climbed back into bed and turned my back to Jared. He wiggled upon me, lightly placing his arm around my waist. Afterwards he kissed me softly on the cheek. I was surprised because he hadn't given me much attention. I didn't move for fear that would cause him to move. It was heaven having Jared beside me to cuddle. One last kiss, and we drifted off into a peaceful sleep. Maybe he wasn't cheating on me.

At 7:15, Jared was out of bed and in the shower. He left his cell phone on the nightstand and it was buzzing. The devil on my shoulder told me to look at the caller ID to see who was calling. The angel on the other side reminded me I didn't want to know. I closed my eyes, trying to regain that peaceful state of sleep that had held me for a couple of hours. The phone buzzed again. I couldn't resist. Truth be told, I didn't want to resist. I wanted to know who was calling Jared so early in the morning. This was a perfect way to find out if I could trust him, without making him aware of my doubts. If there was nothing in his phone, then I would never look again.

I rationalized for at least thirty seconds, which is precious time when you are trying to sneak through your boyfriend's phone while he's in the next room. I took a quick glance toward the bathroom, listening to make sure the shower was running. It appeared to be safe so I grabbed the phone and swiped left. I knew better than to go to his call logs. All guys were hip to deleting incriminating calls, so I touched the text icon to open his messages. I hoped he was stupid enough to let his texts slip through the cracks, just like he was dumb enough not to have his phone locked.

I saw a message that was time stamped for around midnight. His message asked if he could see the person. There was no name stored with the number, which was suspicious to me. My heart thumped. I slid my fingers over the buttons. The number replied at 1:05 A.M.: COME ON OVER. I'LL BE WAITING.

The shower snapped off so I hit the side button, praying the backlight would go off before he finished drying himself. By the time he turned the knob to come out, I was back on my side, head under the covers, with closed, blinking eyes. It was hard to be calm. I wasn't ready to confront him because I wasn't sure if I could handle the truth. I loved Jared. There was so much time invested. I wasn't ready to be set free when the truth reared its ugly head.

Jared walked over to the bed and pulled the blanket back.

"Baby," he said in his deep, sultry voice.

It's amazing how these eyes of love were blind like justice. I started out despising this guy, now he was in control of this relationship. I was losing.

"Baby," he said one more time.

I didn't move so he kissed my forehead and gently shook me. I could have melted into the sheets, like a red crayon on a hot day. I rubbed my eyes and blinked really hard, as if I were in a dead sleep. I may have overdone the sleep act a bit but I didn't let up. He leaned in to kiss me. Normally I would have kissed him back, but I was pissed about the messages. I told myself I couldn't be mad right now. I knew I needed more time to investigate the situation without making him aware of what I was trying to do. I had to think quick before my emotions took over.

"My breath is kicking babe; this is for your own good." I laughed and pushed him away as I got up to head for the bathroom sink.

On the inside, I was burning up!

"I don't care about your breath. I just wanna wake you up the way you deserve, with a kiss. I'm ordering breakfast. How does Ray's Place sound?"

"You know I love Ray's Place. Order the usual for me," I said, brushing my teeth.

I was a crayon in heat. Jared really knew how to push my buttons. He worked so hard to make me happy. Maybe I was reading too much into the texts. I decided to dismiss checking up on him. If he was cheating, his behavior would be different. When he was around, there was no doubt he loved me.

The nightstand vibrated, both Jared and I turned to look around. It was my phone. The private calls were coming more frequently. I hoped it wasn't Omar because I'd worked so hard to keep my number out of his hands. I hit the ignore button like I normally did and set the phone back on the nightstand.

"Who was that?" I heard a tinge of jealousy.

"Oh no, honey, we play by your rules. You don't ask me and I won't ask you, right? You made that rule, I didn't." I smirked when I gave Jared a dose of his own medicine.

Rule number one: I was never to question him about who called his phone. Ever. And he would respect me just the same. So far, Jared had kept his word. There had been nights when I would get a late call from one of my homegirls and purposely not answer it. The most he would do is frown, but he never complained. Today, he caught me off guard with his question, but I was quick on my feet with a comeback.

Kimberlee

Twelve weeks after I promised my husband I would have a
baby, I was peeing on a plastic stick. My period was still coming
regularly, but I was always hungry, nauseous, or both. My nipples
were sore, and my belly was slightly poking out. Even with my
period, the symptoms were cause to test. A plus sign means my
marriage and money are safe. Minus sign meant I had to keep
trying. I put the stick on the bathroom counter and left it there
until I was ready to look.

When I went back, there was a plus sign. Me, plus Big Doc
equals a baby. I didn't know whether to be happy or sad. My
marriage would be saved, but my body would be ruined. I was
willing to take that chance; a plastic surgeon could make me right
if it came down to that. I wanted some wine, but those days were
over, so I settled for sparkling grape juice.

I cried for two days. I didn't know what to do. Lord knows,
I'm not mother material. I didn't have time for a child. Honestly,
I wanted a baby like I wanted a hole in my head. I only agreed to
do this to save my marriage; there was no other way. I couldn't
tell my husband yet. It was too soon and I was still upset. Telling
Big Doc had to be a positive experience. Alicia was my only hope.
I hadn't talked to her in a while, but she was always there when I
needed her. I called her to meet for lunch, and she agreed. Alicia

would be able to comfort me, even more, she could help me find out who my husband was seeing on the side. She'd hired a private investigator on that no-good Omar, and I wanted her to do the same thing for me.

On the flip side, I didn't want Alicia that far in my business. I'd told her about my suspicions of him cheating, but she didn't know he'd admitted it. Therefore, I decided to hold off on the P.I. for a while. The plan was to look into it more on my own. If my personal search didn't bring answers, then I'd call Alicia for Plan B. The first thing I did was bought some of the key stroke counting software. Once I had access to everything he'd been doing on the computer, maybe it would bring clues. I could also use the software to get his Facebook password. Meanwhile, I was doing everything to see the bright side of this pregnancy. I had to tell Big Doc before I got even bigger.

The privacy invading software didn't turn up any results. I guess my husband was too smart to do anything on the computer in the den. I'm sure he was using his laptop for any dirt. There was no doubt that it would cost him dearly if I could prove infidelity in divorce court. One mistake would turn into one big payoff for me. I could live with that, but I'm not sure he could. Then again, merely knowing someone had his attention left me yearning to be with him. Maybe I did love him as much as I loved his money. Only time could tell that.

After the software, I searched credit card statements, bank statements, and call detail on our phone bills for any clues. There were none. Either my husband lied about his affair or he'd carefully covered his tracks. Finally, I decided to call in the big dog.

Alicia picked up the phone without hesitation when I called. I'd been avoiding her lately, and I'm sure she knew, but that's how it was with us. She always had my back. We met at an out-of-the-way restaurant. She kept insisting that I have a glass of wine with her. I refrained from being rude but Alicia was aggravating me. I didn't want to make her mad before I asked her to hire the P.I. for me. I'd thrown on an oversized sweat shirt to hide my bulge, because it was too soon for me to reveal the baby situation. But she kept forcing wine on me until irritation pushed the words through my lips.

"Alicia, I'm pregnant."

Her jaw dropped to the floor. I continued by telling her about the confrontation, then I asked about her friend, Jefferson, the private investigator.

Alicia

I was showing a house on the east side of town when Kimberlee decided to call. I didn't want to be unprofessional, but I had to answer because she'd been missing in action. I told the Brown family to take a second walk-through of the property without me. They agreed they could use the privacy. I rushed out to the deck and hurriedly answered the phone.

"Hello," I said, out of breath.

"Hey, cousin." Kimberlee's voice didn't sound the same.

She was not her usual chipper self, but she asked me to meet her for lunch. She said she needed to talk to me. Considering the circumstances, I told her I would be there.

"One more thing," she rushed out.

"What's that?"

"I don't want to meet at Winky's or Mary Love's. Let's meet some place we ordinarily don't eat; somewhere out of the way. I don't want to see any familiar faces."

It didn't matter to me where we went. I wanted to see Kimberlee.

Kimberlee showed up in a pair of frumpy, sweat-pants and a big sweat shirt. She had a pony-tail, and no make-up. I knew she was upset, but I didn't know she was feeling this bad. She greeted me with a slim smile as she sat down at the table.

"Hey, cousin."

"How's it going, chick?" I asked, knowing full well it couldn't be good.

"I'm cool."

"No, seriously."

It took Kimberlee a few minutes to respond. The waitress arrived to take our orders before she could get it out. We told her we needed a while longer to decide on our entrees, but I asked her to bring two glasses of wine.

"No. No…. Miss, please make that one glass of wine. I'll have water," Kimberlee told the waitress.

The waitress nodded and walked away.

"What's all that about, Kimberlee? We always have wine with lunch."

"I'm having water, Alicia. Please don't question me."

She was snapping at me. I didn't understand why, nor did I allow her to continue.

"Uh, Kimberlee, let's not forget you called and invited me to lunch. I can tell you're going through some tough times, and I intend to stick by your side, helping you however I can. You have my one hundred percent support, but you better watch your mouth. Last I checked, you didn't have any children, so don't talk to me like I'm a child."

"You're right, Alicia. I'm tripping. I've just been dealing with a lot. This thing with Eddie Lee is much deeper; it's killing me, and my head is not right." She shrugged her shoulders, looking at me with her puppy dog eyes.

I felt bad for her. Her body language said she was truly going through it. The only concern I had was narrowing down what "it" was.

Kimberlee filled me in over lunch. She twirled her food around her plate, but didn't eat much. She told me she'd confronted Eddie Lee about his affair, and he'd had the nerve to confirm her suspicions without batting an eye. She was detached from the conversation as she told me he'd admitted to the affair but he'd refused to name his mistress. To take the cake, he'd blamed Kimberlee for his disloyalty. By the time she told me that part, she'd started to break down. She was an emotional wreck, but I understood why.

Can you believe he'd been cheating on her because he wanted a baby? I'd heard my cousin say time after time, she'd never give birth, because of the monstrosities on my belly. Not to mention, Kimberlee wasn't mother material. She surprised me when she told me she was going to have a baby to save her marriage. Meaning, she was already pregnant, that's why she looked so frumpy. I finally understood why she wouldn't have a glass of wine with me. I couldn't believe she was going to go through with it. I told Kimberlee I'd be right beside her, the whole way. Whatever we had to do to save her marriage was fair play.

Kimberlee said she needed professional help finding out who the mystery woman was. Women's intuition told her it was Shontay. I didn't think Eddie Lee would stoop so low, but Kimberlee was convinced. I wondered why she'd be dumb enough to believe her husband would screw a slut maid. Kimberlee hadn't been all that innocent when they met, but she was far from being like Shontay.

I had a private investigator friend, whose agency was a hop, skip, and a jump from my office. I told Kimberlee I'd get him on the job.

We said our goodbyes and I jumped in my ride, heading home. Kimberlee's pregnancy was on the forefront of my thoughts. It made me miss my own son even more. Days like this made me rethink my decision to give him up. It seemed to me I was hurting myself more than Omar.

It was almost forty-five minutes later when I made it home to my wine and weed. I hated to admit it, but I was addicted. Once I had a little of each, I made a call to Jefferson Carter's office. I told him what I knew about Kimberlee's situation. He assured me he could handle it. I was positive I'd hear from him soon. Jefferson had done some work for me before, and he did a good job. It took him three days to track Omar down when he left me and our son without a trace. He'd moved from the apartment he was renting during the course of our relationship, changed his number, and disappeared. I'd never met his mother or any of his family, so I couldn't contact them to reach Omar, who left me the same day our son was born. I cried for two weeks before I called Jefferson for help. I didn't understand how Omar left so effortlessly until Jefferson laid it all on the line for me.

As soon as I hung up with Jefferson, Kimberlee called to remind me to hire him. She also asked me to keep her pregnancy a secret because her husband didn't know yet.

Kimberlee's call prompted a string of them. Directly following our conversation was three private calls. Plus, Jared called to tell me I would be eating dinner alone. For the umpteenth time he wasn't going to be home until late. I was disappointed again to be spending the night without him. I'd planned to have a nice, romantic dinner by candlelight. I wasn't sure what I was going to prepare, but it didn't matter because Jared had ruined it. Mrs. Young called to set an appointment for the following week. I wasn't quite sure what she wanted. I could only hope this was for business.

Alicia

The meeting with Mrs. Young swooped upon me fast. She wanted me to find a three-bedroom, two-bathroom home she could renovate for rental property. As she talked, I noticed her steal an occasional glance at my son's picture, which decorated my desk. She all but picked up the frame. I'm not sure why she never noticed the photo before, but today it stood out to her and she made it obvious.

"That your boy?" She asked as she stood to leave.

"Yes ma'am," I answered, tears forming.

She nodded, abruptly changed the subject, and told me she would be in touch. I'm uncertain how, but it seemed Mrs. Young knew I was uncomfortable.

When Mrs. Young left, I made a call to Jefferson's office. It had been a week or so since I'd hired him for Kimberlee. I'd been talking to her every day since she told me of her pregnancy, so I knew she was anxious for news. Jefferson's secretary put me right through.

"Alicia! Your ears should have been ringing because I was just about to call you." He spoke into the receiver without saying hello.

"I must be psychic, and hello to you," I said with a chuckle.

"I'm sorry, I got ahead of myself, but I'm excited because I've got information concerning your friend, the doctor."

I groaned. Yes, I'd called and asked Jefferson for help, but I wasn't ready to face someone else's truth when I could barely face my own. Besides, I didn't want to have to break the news to Kimberlee, myself.

"Can you hang on the line a second? I want to get Kimberlee on here. She's the paying client, and I don't want her to miss a word. Nor do I want to repeat it."

"Okay but before you talk to Kimberlee, I have something I want to discuss with you. Got a second?"

"Sure. What's up Jefferson?"

"Well technically, I shouldn't discuss this with you but because I know you so well I want to get your advice."

"Go for it," I said, encouraging Jefferson to continue. It seemed to me he was stalling and I was ready to get this over with.

"I have a little suspicion that your friend Tomeka is one of Eddie Lee's mistresses. Yes, he has several but I won't get into that until Kimberlee's on the line. I don't have solid evidence of Eddie Lee and Tomeka but she's showing up in his phone records quite a bit and I have pictures of them together on a couple of occasions. I don't want to tell Kimberlee until I know for certain. But, I'd like to know what you think of the situation. Should I dig further?"

"My goodness, Jefferson. I couldn't imagine Tomeka doing something like that but that doesn't mean she wouldn't. By all means, find out what's going on. I will cover the expenses for the new job so bring me the information and I will decide how to handle it. I'm praying to God that Tomeka hasn't crossed the line. I'm going to go ahead and get Kimberlee on the phone."

"Okay."

I clicked over and dialed Kim's number.

"What's up?"

"Hey, girl. Jefferson is on the other line. If you can talk, I'll beep him in."

Silence.

"Kim, are you ready?"

"Can't be nothing but ready. I asked for this, right?"

"Right. Hold on."

I added Jefferson to our call and let him do the talking. He gave Kimberlee the same run-down he'd given me when I hired him: name, phone number, age, race, and address. She screamed, then hung up on us. I redialed Jefferson to tell him I would drop a check by his office for his services. He thanked me for the referral and told me he would see me soon. I called Kimberlee back. She didn't answer the phone. I called back a second time because she owed me for Jefferson's bill. I decided to give her some time. I would catch up with her later. She could pay me then.

I picked up my cell to call Jared. I missed spending time with him. I wanted Jared to take me out. It was time for us to have the talk that all brothers dreaded - the piss or get off the pot speech. My cell rang before I could finish dialing; it was another private call. Tired of evading, I answered.

"Hello."

"I'm tired, bitch."

Click.

The helicopter rotors beat in my chest again, only this time they were ripping my heart to shreds. I was shocked. It was Michelle, Omar's wife. I knew the shrill of her voice. She had the nerve to call me with the same words I'd written on the note to Omar when I dropped our son off at their house.

Two years ago, Jefferson called and told me he had some pretty disturbing news for me. He didn't want to get into it over the phone. I searched my mind trying to figure out what I'd missed with Omar. I had only asked Jefferson to find him for me, so I wasn't expecting any news, disturbing or otherwise. I panicked for a second, thinking Omar had somehow met his demise. Maybe that was the reason he'd disappeared on us without cause. Unsolicited tears covered my face as I explored that possibility. It was weird because somewhere deep inside, my pride wanted him to be dead. That would be easier than having to face the rejection of him not wanting to be with us. I shook my head, erasing the thoughts like an Etch-a-Sketch. I didn't want Omar dead. I loved him, and he loved me. There had to be a logical reason for his desertion.

Jefferson was outside of his workplace smoking a cigarette when I arrived. The lines on his face told me I wouldn't like what he had to say. Once inside, he walked over to the coffee-pot that was heating in the waiting area and poured a cup of the brown liquid into a medium-sized Styrofoam cup.

He raised the cup to me, "Coffee?"

I shook my head. There was no way I could stomach anything at the moment. My belly was full of butterflies. I was ready to get to the heart of the matter.

He took a sip of his coffee then looked me in the eyes, "Your baby's daddy…"

He took another sip of his coffee, paused and gave me a nervous smile.

"Spit it out." I couldn't stand the suspense.

"Your baby's daddy, Omar Tyrell Walker, is married with children. They live across the bridge on Math Lane. 108 Math Lane, to be exact. He has a seven-year old son and a five-year-old daughter. His wife's name is Michelle, and to be honest, she looks a lot like you."

I was too shocked to move. I wanted to kill Omar. I wanted to pierce his heart with a knife, stabbing him over and over and over until his black ass was no longer moving. His pain should be equivalent to mine.

Visions of a snotty-nosed little girl with pig-tails and Dora the Explorer pajamas danced in my head. I thought about the little boy, who probably resembled my son. I threw up where I stood. I couldn't kill Omar. It wasn't his kids' fault he was a lying, cheating, two-timing dog, not worthy of the air he breathed. I couldn't believe it was happening to me.

I devised a plan of attack in the fifteen-minute drive to my home. I stuffed diapers, formula, and other small knick-knacks into a baby bag, wrote a three-word note on a single piece of paper, and stuffed it in the bag. I cuddled and kissed my son for a few hours before I made that dreadful journey to Math Lane. Along the way, I searched for a pay phone. When I finally found one, I dialed the number I'd been given by Jefferson to be sure someone was home. That was the first time I heard her voice.

"Hello, Walker residence."

I hung up. I hated her immediately. It hurt to hear her answer her phone the way I should have been answering mine. She sounded so happy. She had no clue I was about to rock her world with no remorse.

I bravely knocked on the door of their two thousand square foot home, holding Little Omar's carrier, tears creating a torrential downpour. I didn't plan to go in. I wanted Omar to open the door because I wanted to see the frightful look on his face when he saw me standing there with his illegitimate son. After the satisfaction it brought me, I would give him the carrier and walk away, leaving him alone with his wife to explain the baby he was holding.

I choked when Michelle opened the door. My mouth didn't move at all. I stood there like a deer caught in headlights. Even though she'd answered the phone, I didn't expect her to come to the door. She was a very beautiful woman, and like Jefferson suggested, bore a striking resemblance to me.

"Hello," she said smiling.

"Hi," I stammered. "Um, my car stalled outside and my cell is dead. May I use your phone to call for help?"

It wasn't the most original story, but like I said, I choked. She was as kind as she was pretty because she invited me, a complete stranger, in to use the phone. I was impressed enough to leave without telling her about Omar's transgression. But she pissed me off when she had the nerve to treat me like she felt sorry for me. It made me feel like I was beneath her. I didn't like the way she looked at me. Her sympathy pissed me off. My jealousy made me hate her. I hated her happiness and all of the family photos with the cheesy smiles that were plastered on the walls of their immaculate home. Building blocks and other kid-friendly toys neatly arranged in a corner reminded me I was there to ruin her day.

Out of the blue, I asked about Omar, "Where's your husband?"

She stopped smiling. "Excuse me?"

"That's your husband, Omar, in all the pictures, right?"

I wanted her to deny she was married to him. Despite everything in the home that screamed happy family, I held on to the possibility Omar wasn't her man.

She gave me a shallow smile before she answered me, "Yes, I'm Mrs. Omar Walker."

I laughed, cackled like Mrs. Young did in my nightmares. Hate consumed me.

"Well, Mrs. Omar Walker, meet your step-son."

Her jaw dropped.

"Close your mouth. It's true." I smirked.

Michelle looked in the carrier for the first time since she'd opened the door. She peeled the blanket from around him, gazing for a while.

"Wait here, don't leave," she said calmly as she walked down the hallway to a back room.

I was nervous. Honestly, I wanted her to be hysterical. It scared me that she wasn't, but I waited. She returned with an eight-by-ten photo of her son as an infant, and held it to my baby's face.

"Twins," she said barely audible.

"Huh?"

"Your son… He looks like Omar Jr., spitting image," she said as the first tears made themselves known. "This explains a lot."

She leaned over the carrier, unbuckling my son, "What's his name?"

"Omar," I humbly replied. She was so nice, I felt bad. This wasn't her fault. She was a victim like I was.

"Omar," she repeated giving one of those gotta laugh to keep from crying laughs. "Another Omar, my Lord. Does my husband know?" she asked cuddling my son.

"He knows," I said, walking toward the door. "Do me a favor, give your husband the note that's in the bag; I'll be back."

I couldn't torture her any longer. In a way I was glad I was able to watch her hold my baby. She was a sweet lady; she wouldn't hurt him. She loved him immediately because she loved her husband. Instantly she loved her illegitimate step-son more than My Dear ever loved me. It was painful to watch but I took a fleeting last glance before I let myself out, quietly closing the door.

I was definitely My Dear's daughter. There was no denying that when I didn't go back. Instead, I changed my number and spent the next few weeks holed up in a hotel. Not long after that I moved to a different part of town. I thought about my son every day, but I lived as if he and Omar didn't exist. I hadn't heard a word from either of them until I saw Omar at Mary Love's a while back. Come to think of it, that's when the private calls had started.

Now his wife was calling me. Reality set in. They'd found me. I didn't know if I should be happy or sad. All I knew is I wanted to see my son.

Tomeka

We met at an out of the way hotel. When I say out of the way, I mean an hour away from our home where neither of us knew anybody.

Eddie Lee arrived with a dozen roses. Immediately, I wanted to slip right out of my panties. I couldn't remember the last time Malik had done anything so nice.

"Thank you," I said accepting the arrangement. "They're beautiful."

Eddie Lee smiled. "Beautiful roses for a beautiful lady."

He was flattering me again. Oh how I longed to be in his arms. I smiled at him. He gave me a nervous chuckle. He confessed to me that he'd dreamed about me many nights, as he gently caressed my face.

I needed new panties. My whole body tingled. I knew it was wrong, but I wanted him to touch me everywhere. I opened my mouth to ask for more, but the words wouldn't come. This was wrong.

I told him to stop.

"Stop. Please."

His phone rang before he spoke. He silenced the ring. It rang back instantly and he shut it down again. I couldn't help but wonder if it was Kimberlee calling. A tinge of jealousy invaded me. Jealousy left quickly once he spoke.

"You called me here to save you, Tomeka. Let me save you."

Eddie Lee kissed me hard on the lips. Like an oxymoron, it hurt so good. How did I get myself into this situation? It didn't matter. I kissed him back. He pressed his body against me enough for me to feel his nature rise.

This had gone too far. I broke away from our kiss, grabbing the roses from the hotel nightstand.

"No, Eddie Lee. Go home to your wife. Work it out. Give her these roses. She deserves them."

His blank stare revealed confusion.

I'd only dreamed of being with Eddie Lee. It wasn't really supposed to happen. I wasn't trifling enough to sleep with my friend's husband. Or was I?

I kissed him again before speaking.

"As bad as I want you, I could never completely betray Kimberlee. You made a vow to God. Try to work it out with her. Go home and make love to her as if she's me."

Eddie Lee sat down on the bed, holding the roses. He looked wounded and ashamed. He took a deep breath, then exhaled.

"You're a beautiful woman, Tomeka. Inside and out, you're beautiful. You deserve better than Malik."

I wiped my tears with both hands. Eddie Lee was right. I deserved better… but so did Kimberlee.

He held my hand for a moment. Then he spoke softly, "Are you sure you want me to go?"

Inside I screamed emphatically. *Noooooooooo!*

"Yes, Eddie Lee. Your wife needs you."

His phone rang again. Again he silenced it before he turned to leave. Roses in hand, Eddie Lee took an exit out of my life even faster than he'd arrived. I blew him a kiss before closing the hotel door.

Kimberlee

Not long after I got Alicia on the job, she and the P.I. called to break me down. I'd been right all along. Shontay was sleeping with my husband, but she wasn't my main concern. Jefferson gave the name and address of a woman named Monica Simmons. The name was familiar but I wasn't sure why. It suddenly hit me that she was the stranger who'd friend requested me on Facebook.

I logged into my account to get a feel for who she was. I hoped she was one of those who posted her entire life online. The friend request was no longer there, I was out of luck. Technically, I was fine since Jefferson had given me all of Monica's personal information. I wasn't sure it was a good idea for him to do that, but I was glad he did.

Thinking about everything was giving me a major headache. I popped a couple of Tylenol. Being a doctor's wife, I knew Tylenol wouldn't harm my unborn child. The craving I had for wine was getting stronger and stronger. Sparkling grape juice wasn't cutting it - I needed something stronger. Instead, I settled for a long, hot bath. I fired up the jets on our whirlpool bathtub, lit some candles, and sank deep down under the soothing feel of the bubbles. A relaxing soak wasn't the equivalent of wine, but it took the edge off.

Slumped down in my tub, under a mountain of globe-shaped, air-filled film known as bubbles, my mind wouldn't rest. I wasn't worried about the hubby. I knew I was handling my business with him. The three pair of Christian Louboutin's that showed up on my doorstep in an unmarked box today told me so. Eddie Lee hadn't sent me a gift in ages, so when the shoes arrived, I knew we were back on track. I'd fired Shontay so there was no reason for me to worry about her. My main issue was the mystery woman, Monica Simmons, the woman who'd agreed to give my man a child. My husband continually assured me his little rendezvous with her was over, but I needed to be one hundred percent certain. Maybe I would step to her like Alicia did Omar's wife; walk right up to that hussy's door and confront the situation head on. I was discombobulated and my head was still throbbing. There was no way I wouldn't do something about it.

An hour later, I was zooming down the interstate in my Tom Ford sunshades, windows down, air conditioner on arctic blast, headed for Fianna Estates. My head still hurt, the butterflies in my stomach were dancing, and I didn't have a clue what I planned to do when I saw this woman. Even worse, I didn't know what she would do. I wondered what she would look like, how she would react, and I hoped she wasn't a nice, frilly bitch like Omar's wife. I didn't want to be let into her home. I wanted to fight, but then again, I knew I couldn't fight because I couldn't run the risk of harming our baby. I had to remain calm, maybe befriend her, turn the tables on her. I wasn't sure.

1735 Fianna Estates:

I practiced several speeches for thirty minutes before I approached her door. I shot out of the car like a caged rabbit but walked to the door like a turtle. I had to take my time and do this the right way, but first I had to throw up. The butterflies got the best of me and I had to release them. I dropped my head down behind some of the shrubbery in front of her door and let it all out. I eased back onto the sidewalk, almost turned and went back to the car. Then I realized this was something I had to do so I reached up and rang the doorbell. She opened the door.

"I've been expecting you."

I was perplexed.

"Excuse me?"

"Kimberlee Washington, right? The wife of Dr. Washington, I presume."

I was floored.

"Do come in, Mrs. Washington. I would like to talk to you as much as you would like to talk to me. I've been waiting for months to meet you. I figured you would have shown up here well before today."

I looked at her long and hard before I entered her home. This was not the way things were supposed to be. I wanted to surprise her, not the other way around. Hell, I'd even pondered pretending to be at the wrong address once I'd caught a glimpse of her. I thought I would have the option to walk away, leaving her confused, but I was wrong.

Dead wrong.

She wasn't the most attractive woman I'd seen. She was low man on the totem pole in the looks department compared to me and Shontay. I knew by her shoes, she wasn't a diva, but her demeanor told me she wasn't ghetto.

I stepped into her domain.

"Monica Simmons. Humph. I would say nice to meet you, but I'm sure the pleasure is all yours."

"More than you know," she said with too much arrogance.

I wasn't sure what she meant by that, but I wanted to find out. She'd pissed me off, so I needed to slow things down. I needed to take control of this meeting and get rid of her like I came to do. I looked at her again before speaking. Monica was a lot of woman at six feet tall. Her olive complexion didn't quite match her dark eyes, which were slightly slanted. Her face was narrow with two out of place dimples. Something about her was compelling. I was drawn to her immediately, and could see why my husband had been involved with her, even with her flaws.

"Can I offer you a drink?"

She snapped me out of my trance when she spoke.

"This is not a social visit."

"Get to it then, tell me why you're here."

"Let you tell it, you were expecting me. Why do you think I'm here?"

She smirked at me, lit a cigarette, and sat on a bar-stool.

It was hard being in her presence. I wanted to snap. I had a strong urge to break that Amazon down. Instead, I silently reminded myself of the life inside me. A stronger urge calmed me.

I repeated my question, "Why do you think I'm here?"

"Please honey. I don't have time for games. You came to me," she sucked her teeth after taking a long drag of her cigarette.

I coughed to let her know it bothered me. She didn't seem to care. I was getting uncomfortable.

Our eyes locked. She took another puff of the cancer stick. I smiled at that. Each hit put her one step closer to death.

Nervousness exited my body. I got right to it.

"I'm pregnant. Stay away from my husband."

She pulled a glass ashtray across the top of her bar and smashed the end of her cigarette. Her dark eyes grew darker, looking watery, like she was going to cry. She pulled her hard park of menthol smokes out of her purse and raised it to me.

"Mind if I smoke again?"

"Go ahead and kill yourself some more," I said sarcastically.

"Have one?" She shot back.

She laughed out loud like her comment was funny. I wanted to slap her, but I didn't. I just kept my composure.

We locked eyes again. I wanted to get up and walk right out the door, but I didn't want to retreat, so I stared at her until she stopped looking at me.

"Pregnant, huh?"

"Pregnant."

The water in her eyes fell, antagonizing me.

"Don't dare act like the victim here. Don't you dare act like the victim. I'm his wife!"

"You're his wife, but I'm the woman who fills his void, the one who comforts him. I'm the woman who strokes his ego, without costing him a dime. My love is free. Like no charge, without cost. I'm the woman you're not; the woman he loves. He stopped loving you a long time ago."

That stung.

"I'm his wife," I repeated because I couldn't compete with her statements. "Soon to be the mother of his child." I said, trying to defeat her.

"Join the club." A sneer lined her lips.

If I was a fool, I would've believed she was pregnant.

"What are you saying?"

"Join the club."

There was nothing to say. I ran into her like a freight train, jumped in the air full throttle like Jet Li, kicking that bitch dead in her abdomen. I tried to kill her and her bastard baby. At least that's what I wanted to do. I wanted to whip her so bad I saw it, but I didn't. I chose to handle it differently.

"Take a pregnancy test."

"Yeah, like it's that easy. I just happen to have one in the bathroom. Your husband told me you weren't the brightest crayon in the box; I didn't realize how simple you were until you showed up here."

I didn't entertain her insult, "There's a pharmacy around the corner."

Thirty minutes later she was taking the test. I didn't trust her so I watched her pee, then we watched the plus sign appear in the magic little window. The plus sign shattered my heart. She smiled an ugly smile once we'd confirmed she was pregnant. I shook my head, wishing everything I'd just experienced was an illusion. Suddenly, my stomach was queasy, and I needed to release those butterflies again. I rushed to the toilet, then flushed them away. When the sickness subsided, I was angry.

Once again, she smirked, then pulled the same hard pack of cancer sticks from her purse, tapped the pack, removed a cigarette and dangled it between her lips. She offered me one. This time I took it and put it between my quivering lips. The tears were unstoppable.

I stood inches from her face, whispering to her this wasn't the last she would see of me. I was fit to be tied as I raced out the door. I settled into the seat of my car and took one last drag of that deadly tobacco-filled paper, then smashed it out in the ashtray.

After the incident with Monica, I had to have a glass of wine. I shouldn't have done it, but I stopped at the liquor store before going home. I sat in the parking lot and drank directly from the bottle. I couldn't wait. I drank as much as I could bear then headed home to talk to Big Doc. I dialed his mobile number. Voicemail picked up immediately. I redialed with the same result. If I hadn't just left Monica's house, paranoia would have made me believe he was somewhere with her. Once home, I dialed his number again, this time leaving a message for him to call me as soon as possible. I told him it was urgent.

I didn't know what to do with myself while I killed time in lieu of him coming home. The effects of the wine left my head spinning. I had a decision to make. I could either tell my husband about my pregnancy and hope he would confess to me about Monica's pregnancy or I could confront him with her pregnancy and not mention mine at all.

I finished off the wine, sitting at my kitchen table before I called one last time.

"Hello." He answered quickly, to my surprise.

"Hello, baby," I said, trying to sound calm. I didn't want to give any indication I was upset.

"Is everything okay?"

"Everything's fine. Why wouldn't it be?" I asked.

"You left an urgent message for me to call you."

I'd forgotten just that quickly I had asked him to call me, but I played it cool.

"Oh yeah, I did, huh? I have some exciting news to share with you, when will you be home?"

"I'm on my way now, should be there shortly."

I felt my heart skip a beat. How could he be so nonchalant while there was another woman pregnant with his child? The nerve of this man to play me like this. I was upset, but I kept my composure. "See you then, babe."

Not long after he hung up, I heard the garage whir. Big Doc came strolling in with a dozen white roses, my favorite. My husband greeted me with a long, passionate kiss that reminded me of the good ole, days. He was so sweet that I almost forgot about Monica.

A flutter in my stomach jolted me back to my mission. I wasn't sure if it was the baby or more butterflies. At this point, it didn't matter because the moment of truth was at hand. I picked up the wine glass in front of me and took a long, slow drink from it. I knew I shouldn't be drinking, but I was hoping the wine would calm me enough to have this much-needed conversation with my husband. I wanted to blurt it out, wanted to tell him I was pregnant and so was his mistress, then ask him what he planned to do. The look on his face would be priceless when he realized the severity of the issue. I didn't want to yell and scream, I just wanted to say it all with distinctness. But it wasn't so easy.

After the kiss, he brought me in to him, hugging me like he used to. Then he whispered in my ear how much he missed me. He even called me sexy.

Again, I lost my composure. It had been a long time since he'd made me feel special.

I didn't want to ruin the night with an argument, so I held off on the talk.

"I missed you honey. How was your day?"

I asked him that as I wrapped my arms around his waist. A snug feeling overtook my body as he returned the affection.

"Let's not waste our night talking about the politics of my work day. Let's get down to why you wanted me to rush home to you." He gave a seductive smile as he said those words to me.

Before I could respond, he lifted me up in his arms. I wrapped my arms around his neck as he led us to the bedroom. My husband pushed the bedroom door open with his foot, then tenderly lay me down on our bed. He looked deep into my eyes before placing a string of sensuous kisses up my arm toward my mouth. He parted my lips with his tongue. My body melted into the silkiness of the sheets. Big Doc told me not to move as he begun to remove my clothes, then his own.

Slowly, methodically, he undressed. I looked over his body. He'd always had a nice physique, even back in his nerdy college days. My heart raced and I couldn't wait. He took his time literally not missing one inch of my body with his kisses. I couldn't stand the foreplay; I urged him to enter me.

"Be patient, baby. Enjoy the moment."

He kissed me again. This time, with more passion than ever before. He kissed my lips, then nibbled my tongue, ears, and neck. He kissed me hard some more, and ran his tongue down my stomach toward my thighs, snaking his way to my triangle. I was suddenly hot, intense moans escaped my lips as he massaged my spot. I squirmed and wiggled away, he pulled me back to him, refusing to let me out of his reach. I arched my back, wrapped my arms around his head, and moved my pelvis closer to his face. The warmth of his mouth invaded me until I couldn't take anymore.

"Please make love to me," I begged.

Big Doc shhh'd me, while he continued his mission.

Everything was so tender and emotional. I loved my man. During our love session I became conscious of the fact that Big Doc was still a good man. In fact, he was a wonderful man, a better man than I deserved. It was getting hotter in the bedroom. I decided to share the pleasure with him so I pulled him up to me, forcing him onto his back. He liked when I was forceful because it heightened his arousal. I gave him my tongue, like he did me. My husband looked at me with the heat that I'd been feeling, now in his eyes.

He screamed out as he reached his climax.

"Oh Tome-. Oh to me you are the most beautiful woman in the world." I could have sworn he almost said Tomeka, but I had to be tripping. I gave him a once over. He didn't flinch. So I knew he hadn't slipped up.

He lay there beside me, naked, and running his hands through my wavy, coal-black hair.

"I know things have been strained lately, but I want you to know I love you, honey."

"I love you, too"

"Now, tell me what was so urgent?"

"The fire you put out."

He smiled.

Neither of us moved again, until he left for work.

Alicia

I tried to call Jared. We needed to talk. There was a lot he didn't know about the situation with Omar and my son, and if I was going to repair our relationship, I couldn't blindside him.

Phone in hand, I dialed Jared's number again. It bothered me that he didn't answer the phone because I was anxious to talk to him. Kimberlee and Tomeka were my next options. Maybe I could get them to meet me at Mary Love's. Neither of them answered.

I headed to Mary Love's alone. Once inside, I ordered a personal pizza and a bucket of Budweiser's. A few of my biker buddies, the City Ryders, were there, so I was able to trade my pain for a good time. Truth be told, I wanted to vent to my girls, but for now I would settle for the City Ryders. I partied for hours, this time hoping Omar would be there. I'd avoided Mary Love's since my run-in with him. I couldn't shake the humiliation of not being able to handle him that night. In the beginning of our relationship, I was the bomb at keeping him in check. Yet, I allowed him to steal my *oomph*. To my dismay, Omar never showed. I staggered out of the bar toward my car, around two in the morning. I could barely walk, but I planned to drive myself home. A knock on the window startled me. It was Tomeka's man, Malik. I couldn't imagine what he wanted. I rolled the window down to find out.

"What's up Malik?"

"I can't let you drive home, Alicia. You're twisted."

"I'm fine," I said, slurring my words.

"Hell no, I can't let you do it. My man, Trey is going to follow us, and I'm going to drive you."

I didn't protest. Malik drove me home, then hopped in the car with Trey. I watched them drive away. Trey was fine. He'd make a nice replacement for Jared. It was too bad he had his woman in the car with him.

I staggered in the house, only to realize Jared wasn't there. I debated with myself about breaking up with him. As far as I was concerned, I didn't have to go through this with Jared. But every time I was ready to call it off, he would do something really sweet. On most occasions, he was barely attentive to me, or downright rude. It was hard to tell if he loved me or hated me, but I stayed around because of the few times he seemed to care. When I finally told him of my plans to get my son back, he was very supportive, even offering to help with the legal fees. My heart melted when he offered. It was like old times, back when I knew he had my back. The day he did that, I'd planned to give him an ultimatum concerning our relationship, but the conversation never made it there.

Even though I was in a drunken stupor, I smoked a blunt and drank some more, practicing in the mirror what I would say to Jared.

"Jared, honey. You know I love you, right?" I laughed at myself because I sounded like a guest on one of those trashy, daytime talk shows. I could hear the audience screaming "Jerry! Jerry! Jerry!" I decided to change it up. There was no reason to beat around the bush. I would be straight up.

"Jared, I love you, but this relationship isn't working. I need time and attention. I realize you're busy, but if you don't have time for me, I'm done. It hurts more than it feels good, and love shouldn't be that way. How am I eating and sleeping alone when we live together? You've changed and with you, our relationship has changed. You either love me or you don't, either way I have to know."

I recited my speech several times before I called him because it had to sound natural.

"Hey baby!" He answered, excitedly. That's exactly what I've been complaining about. Whenever I have my nerves up to talk, he seems to care. It's like he has a sixth sense about it.

"Can you come home? We need to talk." I was straightforward with Jared. I had to stick to my guns. I didn't want him to change my mind this time. We'd needed to have this talk for a while now.

"I was just about to call to tell you that I can't make it home, but I need you to do me a favor."

"Typical. How selfish can you be Jared? I'm getting- - - "'

"Be quiet and listen for a change. I need you to do me a favor, then we'll talk."

I was fuming.

"What? What? What?"

"Do you have an attitude?"

"No, I don't have an attitude. Lord knows I don't have a reason to be upset," I said, cynically.

He totally ignored my comment.

"Look in my drawer, there's a black sock in there with about four grand inside."

I instantly fired questions at him like a torpedo. "Four thousand dollars? Are you doing something illegal? Why else would you have four thousand dollars lying around? I don't want no part of this Jared."

"Chill out a second and listen to me."

He was getting irritated, so I did as I was told.

"Take the money, then go to the computer desk. There is an envelope under the keyboard with your name on it. Inside that envelope is an airline ticket to the A-T-L. Take a G and go shopping for yourself. Bring the rest of the money to Atlanta.

Your plane leaves at four. I'll be at the airport waiting for you. Got it?"

"Got it."

Jared was in control again, just like that. Everything I'd planned to say went right out the window. I passed out, only to wake up rushing to pack for my trip to Atlanta.

Alicia

Jared picked me up from the airport right on time. Ego and pride oozed from his pores, I could feel it in the air. I smiled uncontrollably when I noticed him in the driver's seat of a late-model Mercedes CLK 500. It had a shiny black exterior, peanut butter interior, and chrome wheels. The cherry air freshener was overwhelming enough to make me sick, someone obviously sprayed too much.

Jared looked good, nothing like the saggy, baggy elephant I'd grown accustomed to. He was sporting a cream-colored linen suit with tan gator dress shoes. Sultry jazz instrumentals poured from the satellite radio. I was in Heaven. I leaned the seat back to relax a bit as we drove in from the airport. I'd allowed jetlag to whip my butt. My mind was in a euphoric state until it hit me that Jared never listened to anything other than rap. I raised my seat up a little, watching him through one eye. I was baffled by his sudden interest in jazz, but I didn't want to think any further about it. Maybe this meant Jared was maturing. I adjusted my seat again, and pushed the negative vibes away.

I didn't rest long. I was sitting straight up before we bent the next curve. I was too taken aback by the whole scenario to sleep. My mind raced. Something was off. How did a guy who worked at Target afford to fly me to Atlanta? When did he start listening to jazz? And whose car were we soaring down the interstate in?

Leaning forward once more, I couldn't resist. I had to ask Jared at least one question.

"What's this all about baby?" I asked, curiously.

With his eyes on the road and one hand on the steering wheel, he used his free hand to pull a piece and chain from underneath his shirt.

"HBE? What does that stand for?" I asked with a bewildered frown.

"Hustleboy Entertainment, sweetheart. This is our year! Watch and see what I tell you. I found a plug who can get all the acts for the low-low. It's on and poppin' baby. All you have to do is stick with your man. Now, sit back, relax and enjoy the ride."

I couldn't help but smile at Jared. He was amazing. I leaned back in the seat, wondering what he had in store for the night.

I decided to bask in the moment. Rather than asking a bunch of annoying questions, I enjoyed our time together. Jared took me back to our suite at the Marriott where I changed into a short, but classy tan dress that clung to me like plastic wrap. I didn't know where we were headed, but I was determined to look just as good as my man.

After a nice dinner together, we went to The Basement, an elegantly laid hip-hop club in the downtown area. Jared had a key so we entered through the back, near the manager's office. The main level was wall to wall with people. There were two bars, one on each side of the club, and a dance floor in the middle where the crowd exchanged movement, sweat, and body odor. I watched the sultry dancing that took place. The vibe was off the hook. The club owner escorted Jared and me to the actual basement part of the club, where a second deejay mixed. The sound guy checked the mics, as a stage was being set up. I didn't like the way she looked at Jared when they talked. Maybe I was paranoid, but I had a feeling there was more to their relationship than business.

As we walked the club, I noticed several oversized posters advertising Jared's concert plastered all over the walls: HUSTLEBOY ENTERTAINMENT IS IN THE BUILDING! BRINGING YOU THE BEST IN HIP-HOP ENTERTAINMENT. LIVE IN CONCERT: STRAIGHT OUT THE 334, TABIUS TATE: GET READY FOR THE ALABAMA TAKEOVER AND ARKANSAS' FINEST, SACRED YOUNG: HE'S WHAT THE STREETS BEEN WANTIN'! YOU DON'T WANT TO MISS IT!

Toward the bottom of the poster was a full body picture of Jared, sporting the chain that he'd flashed at me in the car. It was like a dream. Not only was he promoting a concert at The Basement. He was bringing two of Hip Hop's hottest new faces with him. One of the artists who'd be performing was Jared's favorite lyricist, Tabius Tate. A new face who was taking the Atlanta club scene by storm. If Tabius Tate was in the house, you better believe the crowd was jumping, especially if he performed *Addicted to the Money*. The other rapper was Sacred Young, who he listened to at every opportunity. Jared always talked about Sacred Young's rugged realness. I could hear him now. "Sacred Young is the truth!" Nobody topped Sacred Young or Tabius Tate in Jared's book and he had them both in concert. It was easy to understand Jared's excitement. As we walked around the club, I started to ooze a little as well.

The owner of the club, Victoria, was an attractive woman with silky, honey colored hair, and caramel skin. She was beautiful. I could tell by looking that she was around forty. Her aura revealed her age, even though she didn't physically look a day over twenty-five. It made me sick that she touched Jared when she talked to him. It was too flirtatious for me. I didn't like the fact that she knew enough about Hustleboy Entertainment to have posters made before I even knew it existed. If I was a gambling woman, I'd bet a million dollars that she listened to jazz. I didn't like Victoria, but I refused to ruin Jared's big night. After all, he'd introduced me as his fiancée so I had no reason to worry. Eventually, she left us alone, but she sipped martinis and watched us all night. I knew she watched us because I kept my eye on her.

The concert was a success. I partied like it was 1999. I was proud of Jared because he pulled it off on the first try, but I was a little taken back by the fact that he'd started promoting concerts without telling me. I racked my brain trying to remember if I'd told Jared about Omar's aspirations to be a promoter. I was ninety-nine percent sure I'd told him, and it bothered me to think he was going out the way to be like Omar. It worried me to think about how far Jared would take his charade. It made me wonder if he was married with a family, too.

The next morning I was alone in our suite. Jared went to the hotel gym to work out, without taking his phone. He'd held so tight to that electronic black book lately, I was sure he didn't realize he left it. I was nervous as I picked it up, but I didn't let the nervousness stop me. This was my only chance to find out if he was cheating. I walked to the room door, making sure it was locked.

The first message I saw was from a naked chic named Ramona. My heart thumped, and I kept scrolling. There was message after message from chic after chic. Finally, I saw what I was truly looking for: texts from Victoria. She missed him, couldn't wait to see him, didn't want to meet me, but was anxious to scope the competition. I couldn't believe my eyes. The last text sealed the deal. It said she'd have the car washed and ready for his arrival. I was hot! We'd been riding around in her Benz. I closed the flip on his phone, then put it back where I found it. I didn't want to see anymore. How much evidence did I need to realize Jared was a Doberman Pinscher?

I was happy I hadn't completely unpacked. I took a shower and threw a few scattered belongings back in my suitcase, stole some of Jared's club money, and hit the road. I was on the next flight out, headed home.

Tomeka

Although I'd only kissed him, I felt guilty about my tryst with Eddie Lee. That guilt spawned a reaction. My relationship was on the line and I had the nerve to meet my friend's husband at an out of the way hotel. Sometimes, I amazed myself with the way I behaved because of Malik. The pain from our issues pushed my desire toward another man. He was always in the streets, never home. Most days he left before noon and we didn't see him again until after midnight. Everything I did irritated him. If I didn't cook, he'd complain. However, the many nights I did prepare family dinner, Malik would have late night leftovers because he was never home in time to sit down and eat with us. Our broken home is definitely Malik's fault.

Oh, who am I kidding? Our relationship was a fairy tale before I changed my life. How could I expect him to change simply because I had? Those were unfair, uncommunicated expectations. I am as much to blame as Malik, because I didn't talk to him about changing. I'd only hoped he would change. To top it off, I almost slept with my friend's husband, when my celibacy was the only reason Malik was creeping. What a hypocrite! I had to make this right.

When I got home to Malik, I told him we could try to work things out. He was ecstatic that I was willing to make an effort toward our relationship. He made a million promises that I knew he wouldn't keep. As I predicted, things with Malik were normal before I could blink.

Things went well initially because he made a special effort to be home more during the day. He was always available for us to have dinner as a family. Even though Malik still spent the majority of the day gone, I appreciated his effort. I tried to understand that he was out making a way for us. I gave him the benefit of doubt, then slowly but surely, family dinner was back down to three.

My cell rang, and it was Malik calling to tell me he wouldn't be home for dinner. He also told me he'd be out late handling business and that I shouldn't wait up. How many nights would I allow him to break his promises to me and the boys?

After dinner, Khalil and Khalik took a bath, then I tucked them in bed. It was "me" time and that meant time for a joint. Although the weed had a calming effect on my nerves, I always felt guilty after I smoked; just not guilty enough to quit.

My cell phone rang. I glanced down at the caller ID. If it wasn't Malik, I had no intention of answering. Deep down, I wanted him to call back to tell me he would be home. I was disappointed to see that it was Alicia calling. I watched her name dance across the screen while I contemplated answering.

"What's up girl?" Alicia asked.

"Nothing much, what's going on with you?"

"I have some things on my mind, and I need some company. Care to join me at Mary Love's?"

"I can't make it tonight, Alicia. I have a ministry meeting with Tina, and I'm not sure how long it will go on," I lied.

It was wrong for me to lie to her, but I wasn't up to sitting in Mary Love's with her while she went on and on about Jared. My love life was in shambles and I'd much rather share that with Tina while we smoked.

"Well, I don't want to interfere with you and church. Guess I'll be heading out alone again tonight. Call me if you change your mind."

"Okay, I'll talk to you later," I said, relieved I was able to get her off the subject so easily.

I called Tina to see if she wanted to hang out at my house for a while. She said she wasn't feeling well and was in for the night. I was disappointed to say the least. Once again, I was home alone with nothing to do and I was tired of it. I called my mama to see if the boys could spend the night. When she agreed I called Alicia and told her I would meet her at Mary Love's.

Alicia spent an hour venting about Jared and some chic from Atlanta. I initially expected her to break down, but she held up surprisingly strong. Her eyes told me she wanted me to say something so I appeased her with conversation about church and God. It was all I had because I hadn't heard much of what she said. She rejected my sermon, and we both laughed because I was trying to preach to her in a bar. What she didn't know was I started talking about God because every time the bar maid passed by, I wanted to grab a drink of my own. I wanted anything, a margarita, some wine, or beer. At this point, any drink would do.

Finally, when I couldn't take it anymore I told Alicia I was going home because I was tired. Mark me down for another lie. The truth was if I stayed another minute, I would've backslid further than I already had. The alcohol was calling my name and so was the weed. Why in the hell would I sit in a bar and not drink when I could sit home and get high as a kite? It was time for me to go. I'd even decided if Malik was home, I'd give him a taste of my goods. I needed some sexual healing. It had been too long. Alicia dropped a bombshell on me before I could make my exit. I wasn't mentally prepared for what happened next.

Alicia

I was restless after leaving the airport. I'd had suspicions that Jared was cheating but knowing for sure was a totally different ball game. I refused to cry. But even if I'd wanted to cry, my tear well was completely empty. Omar depleted it. I was tired of calling my girls and running to Mary Love's every time something was wrong. I didn't know what to do.

I went on a cleaning binge, starting with the kitchen. Nothing was out of place when I finished. I looked at the wall clock. It was early and I was still restless. So much for not going to Mary Love's. I called the clique to see who was down. Kimberlee didn't answer. I made a mental note to make an extra effort to check on her later. We hadn't spoken in a couple of months, and I'd been too absorbed in myself to notice. Shonda simply refused to hang out with me. She'd been acting strange like that lately. In a last ditch attempt, I called Tomeka to meet me. She told me she had a church meeting and couldn't make it, but called back within minutes with a change of plans. Guess it would be just the two of us tonight.

An hour later I was sitting at a slightly battered table, eating pizza and drinking with Tomeka. The outing to Mary Love's was the first step in my healing process. Jared was blowing up my cell phone. There was no need to answer. We were done, and I didn't want to talk about it. During my cleaning spree, I packed his things. I didn't know when to expect him home, but I hoped not to be anywhere around when he showed up.

I filled Tomeka in on my Atlanta trip, told her about the concert and the hoochie, Victoria, who owned the club. She waited for the tears that never surfaced. Eventually, she started talking to me about church and God's plan for me.

"Tomeka, honey, we're in a bar. This isn't the time or place for ministering the gospel." I said, taking a sip of my wine.

"You're right," she laughed.

Seconds became hours. I was having such a good night. It was well after midnight before I noticed the time. Tomeka was sober and not having nearly the fun I was, so she was ready to leave. I told her to give me a second and I would walk her out. I'd just noticed Trey across the room and wanted to thank him for following me home the night I'd been drunk. I even thought briefly about dropping him a note with my number. As I approached him, I halted in my tracks. It appeared to me that Malik was behind Trey at a booth in a very dark far corner with a nasty-looking trick. I stood staring and taking in the scene. Maybe Malik was just having a friendly conversation and I was reading too much into it. I moved off to the side hoping he didn't notice me. Less than a minute later, I saw Malik locking lips with the trick. It was official. My girl's man was cheating on her.

Ironically, she was at the club consoling me because I'd found out Jared wasn't being faithful. I contemplated telling Tomeka. She was too close to the situation not to know. There was no way my friend would be made a fool of. I rushed back to the table where she sat resting her chin in her hands.

"Come here girl, I have something to show you," I told her, grabbing her hand and pulling her out of her seat.

"What is it, Alicia? I'm ready to go home," she said, yawning and sitting back down. "You need to finish whatever you're doing so we can get out of here."

"Believe me girl, you want to see this!"

Tomeka reluctantly trailed me from one side of Mary Love's to the other. A loud gasp and heavy breathing told me when she spotted Malik. I looked back and she'd stopped in her tracks. This time she grabbed my arm, pulling me back toward her. She didn't stop walking until we were in the restroom.

"Tell me that wasn't Malik," she said, tears falling.

"I can't say that T. It was Malik," I said point blank.

There was a moment of awkward silence.

"Do you know the girl?" she asked me.

"She looks familiar but I can't say I know her. Do you?"

"Tina."

"As in your friend from church?" My eyes were big as saucers. "What do you wanna do, girl? I'm in this with you. Say the word, and we kick her ass."

"There's no need for violence. The devil is a lie. The devil is a lie," she took a deep breath, raising her hand to the sky.

She marched out the restroom like Oprah Winfrey in *The Color Purple*. I expected her to say, "You told Harpo to beat me?" It would have been funny if it wasn't such a serious situation. There was no trace of the many tears she'd cried when she reached the dark, far corner where her boyfriend sat kissing her friend from church.

Tomeka approached the table when they were unlocking their lips, catching them red-handed.

"Hey guys, what's up?" Tomeka asked flatly.

Neither of them spoke.

"What's wrong? Cat got your tongue? Oh, wait! There's no way the cat could have your tongues because if that was the case they couldn't have been down each other's throats. Malik, I want you out the house. Matter of fact, don't come home. I'll put your things on the curb. Tina, you're such a hypocrite. I don't have any words for you."

Malik tried to speak, but Tomeka shushed him with her index finger before calmly walking away. I was proud of her. I know for a fact I wouldn't have handled things like she did. I stood there shaking my head at Malik after my friend walked away. I should have been walking with her, but utter shock had me still.

Malik grabbed my arm, "It's not what it looks like Alicia." His eyes pleaded with me.

"I'm not the one you need to explain to," I told him.

I walked over to Tina and slapped her. It wasn't my battle, but I couldn't resist. I tried to slap the black off her face, and then I turned to catch up with Tomeka. I wasn't worried about Tina coming after me.

"The devil is a lie. The devil is a lie." Tomeka was repeating herself.

"Let's get out of here."

She shook her head no.

One of the bar bunnies approached our table with an open bottle of Budweiser. Tomeka gave her a five-dollar bill, and told her to keep the change.

"Don't do it T. You've come too far. Don't let Malik cause you to backslide. You'll regret it in the morning. Don't become the person you've accused Tina of being."

She looked at me through empty eyes.

"The devil is a lie," she said, guzzling the beer.

It hurt to see her do that. Just a few hours earlier she was schooling me on how God would get me through my ordeal with Jared. Now she was sitting in that same chair downing her liquid pain reliever. It was sad to watch because she'd worked so hard at changing her life. One night out brought her full circle. Guilt ate at me like ants at a picnic. If only I would have handled my own issues without involving Tomeka, this wouldn't be happening. On the flip side, she needed to know and I was happy I'd helped her find the truth. I wasn't sure how long she'd been a prisoner to lies. I'm sure there were signs that she ignored, just as I had.

I tried to take her home with me. I didn't want Tomeka to be alone. On top of that, I didn't want to be alone either. You would think I'd be used to my own company by now. Honestly, I was used to being alone, but break-ups are hard on the soul. She declined my invitation. I thought about going home with her, but changed my mind because it was likely that Malik would come crawling in begging and pleading. I didn't want to witness that. My girl needed privacy. I watched her screech out the parking lot, and then I walked slowly to my car.

I hit the alarm button on my key ring as I approached the car. I was surprised to see Trey leaning against my car, looking sexy.

He smiled at me, "That was crazy, huh?"

"Tell me about it," I said.

"I tried to warn that dude. He was here with Tina the last time we were here. I can't believe you didn't see her then. She was in the car when we followed you home."

"I don't know Tina all that well. I've heard her name a million times but never had a face to put with a name. So is that why he insisted on driving me home. Was he trying to feel me out?"

Silence was the indicator that I was right. Malik didn't really care how much I'd been drinking that night. He was looking out for himself.

"Men," I said more to myself than to Trey.

"Not all of us are like that."

"I'll believe it when I see it. In my experiences, yall are all the same."

Trey laughed at me.

"What do you say we get out of this parking lot and grab some grub at an all-night diner?"

"Like I said, men! I'm going home - alone!"

I hopped in my ride, closed the door, and rolled out on Trey, purposely kicking up some of the gravel in the parking lot at him. I wasn't about to become his next victim.

Jared was beside himself when I finally sashayed into our home. He'd caught a late flight out of Atlanta and was home by midnight. I guess he couldn't take what he'd been dishing out for so long. He'd called my phone a million times and left a hundred messages. I deleted them all without listening.

"Why haven't you answered the phone? I've been worried sick," he yelled as soon as I opened the door.

I clutched my chest, made a surprised face, "Oh, excuse me... are you talking to me?"

"You know damn well I'm talking to you, Alicia. You need to stop playing these childish games and tell me what's going on."

I marched past him, headed for the bedroom, where a blunt and my bed should have been waiting.

The blunt was gone. I knew Jared had smoked it before I asked. Somewhere along the way, he'd started smoking weed, too.

"Did you smoke my blunt, Jared?"

"Screw that blunt. I'm trying to talk to you and all you can think about is smoking? What's up Alicia?"

"You tell me," I said, fumbling around my nightstand for my other stash.

Jared slammed the drawer before I could find what I was looking for.

"Talk to me! What's going on?"

Jared was irate, but I didn't care.

"Excuse me Jared," I said tugging on the drawer again. "Will you move your hand? I wanna roll up?"

"I ain't moving!" he snapped.

I didn't feel like arguing. There was no need to. I walked out of the bedroom back to the front. Jared followed so close he stepped on my heels.

I spun around to face him, "Stay off my heels!"

He grabbed me violently, demanding I talk to him.

"You better get your hands off me, Jared. I don't play the domestic violence crap."

I was screaming now. He'd really pushed my buttons when he snatched me by the arm. I grabbed an emergency stash from under the bar, threw it in my purse, then went toward the door.

"Don't walk out on me, Alicia. I mean it." He narrowed his eyes and his breathing thickened.

"Are you sure you meant Alicia? Or is it Ramona? No, excuse me, my bad, it's Victoria. Am I right, Jared?"

Now his chest heaved as he breathed. He didn't speak.

"Ohhhh, so now the cat's got your tongue. That damn cat, he's been taking tongues all night." I laughed, slamming the door.

Jared chased me into the yard.

"Alicia! Alicia!"

"What?"

"One last thing before you go," he said as he raised his hand to me, leaving its print on my face.

Jared slapped me so hard I saw stars. Tears welled in the corners of my eyes. In an instant he realized what he'd done, and became a different person.

"I'm sorry, baby. I'm sorry. I didn't mean to hit you. Please forgive me. You left Atlanta without a word, stole my money, and then wouldn't talk to me, all without an explanation. I'm afraid of losing you. I love you so much, you don't understand."

I looked him in the eyes, took a deep breath, and spit in his face before racing to my car to leave.

Kimberlee

I was asleep on the sofa when I heard the roar of the garage. My heart began to beat excitedly. My husband was home and I was ecstatic, especially after the nights of passion we've shared the past few months. I'd intended to set up a romantic dinner to tell him the news, but he'd come home earlier than normal. I walked into the kitchen to greet my man when he came in. He opened the door with a smile, then covered my lips with his. I felt like I was dreaming. The love I'd been looking for had rekindled right before my eyes. Today was a perfect day to share the news of my pregnancy with him.

"We need to talk," I said when we broke our kiss.

"Let's not waste time talking. I didn't ask Dr. Anderson to cover for me so we could talk. I came home to get some good loving," he said as he wrapped his long arms around my waist and led me to the front of the house.

A half hour later, my husband and I were sandwiched together on the sofa. I heard his cell phone vibrating against the floor. I was immediately irritated because I still hadn't told him about our baby.

"Let it ring," I said.

"I have to answer, honey. It could be the clinic."

"Thought you said Dr. Anderson was covering for you."

"He is."

"Then why do you have to answer?"

"I just have to," he said looking at the screen.

A frown covered his face as he answered the phone. He sat up on the couch and I lay there wrapped in a thin bed sheet, watching his every move. His facial expression changed a million times like a Mr. Potato Head doll. He never said more than "yes, no, or I see". Finally, he ended the call. Then he stood up and started to get dressed.

"What was the phone call about," I asked.

He didn't respond to me, just continued to get dressed.

"Are you leaving? Where are you going?" I asked, confused.

"I'll be back later."

I asked him again where he was going. He told me I didn't want to know the answer. I demanded he tell me what was going on. I wasn't prepared to accept anything less than the truth. Finally, he admitted that the call had come from his mistress, and then he said he was leaving me because she was pregnant and he wanted to be there for his unborn child.

"How could you make love to me and leave me all in the same day? I thought you loved me. I don't understand." I cried uncontrollably as I asked those questions.

"She's pregnant Kimberlee. It's not about you or her anymore. It is about the child that's going to come into this world. She's having my baby and I plan to be there every step of the way."

He was serious. He was going to leave me for that Amazon bitch. I couldn't take it.

"What about me? I'm pregnant, too. This isn't how I wanted to tell you," I cried.

"Don't get weird on me, Kimberlee. You're not pregnant so accept it with dignity, because I'm leaving you regardless."

I raised my shirt to show him the roundness of my stomach. It wasn't much of a pooch, but I was definitely showing.

"You waited too late. She could go into labor any day, and I'm going to be with her."

I couldn't believe my ears. She didn't seem that far along when I saw her. I couldn't tell by looking that she was pregnant. Then again, she was a big woman, which could have hid the pregnancy.

Big Doc pushed me to the side like a used napkin. He went upstairs to grab a few of his things. I sat down on the same sofa we'd just made love on. How could he do this to me? He begged me to have his baby, forced this on me, now he was leaving me to raise this baby alone. Even after I showed him my stomach, he planned to leave anyway. I couldn't take this sitting down; I had to do something.

I made my way up the stairs, into the bedroom with my husband. I begged him not to leave me, told him I would do whatever he wanted me to do. I professed my love on one knee. "Please don't leave baby. Please don't do this."

"What do you want from me Kimberlee? I told you she's due any day now, and I'm going to be there. She called to tell me she's having pains as we speak. I'm going to be there for my child, whether you like it or not."

I didn't like it, nor did I have to accept it. My mind swirled out of control. I was nauseous. I ran to the bathroom, and lost my lunch. The room started to spin and excruciatingly sharp pains shot through my stomach. I screamed out for my husband to help me, only to have him look at me as if I disgusted him.

"I thought you were a classy lady, Kimberlee. This is not funny. It's actually scary to think you'd take such extreme measures to get my attention. I'm leaving. Get over it."

I crawled across the bathroom floor, grabbing his leg.

"Please get me to a hospital before I lose my baby!"

He shook his leg to lose me. He didn't believe I was sick until he saw the puddle of blood beneath me.

It was too late by the time we arrived at the hospital. I'd miscarried. I couldn't believe what was happening. My heart stopped, and my world came to an abrupt end when they gave me the news. It was over for me. I didn't have a chance of keeping my husband.

Big Doc left me as soon as I was stable. I lost my baby and my husband the same day. I didn't know what to do. I spent three days holed up in the house with my dogs. I didn't shower, answer the phone, or leave. I barely even ate.

I called my husband several times a day, every day. The last time he answered, he told me never to call him again because it was upsetting for Monica and he didn't want her to have a mishap with their baby. That was enough for me. I told him I understood and vowed to never call him again.

Once I hung up, I went to the medicine cabinet to retrieve the prescription pain pills from my recent ordeal. The only way I would never call him again is if I wasn't here. I had no reason to live if he wasn't going to be part of my life. I sat on the toilet, writing what would become my final words. I poured the pills into my hand, staring at them. Why did God do this to me? I picked up the pen, added more to the note. I wanted Big Doc to feel guilty once they found me. I ended the letter by telling him he'd made a huge mistake, which cost me my life. I told him this was his fault, talked about how much I loved him and explained how he'd crushed my soul. I hoped he would live with regret for the rest of his life. I wanted him to resent his bitch and her bastard baby, forever. There was no doubt in my mind he loved me. He would never forgive himself.

As I thought about it, I got scared. Death is permanent; there's no coming back from it. Divas don't take themselves out. I'm supposed to have it all. I want my husband and my baby. There was no chance of having my baby, but I was determined to get my husband back. I didn't have any idea what I was going to do. One bad decision and my life is in shambles. I knelt down to pray.

"Heavenly Father, I come to you today on bended knees, with my head bowed and my heart humbled. I know I haven't been the most obedient child of yours, but I'm sure I'm not the worst. I ask you Father to remove this hate from my heart. I hate myself and I hate this life. I beg of you Father to have mercy on me, heal this bruised heart Father God. Then Father, please save me from myself. I need you more than ever, Lord. Help me. Please help me."

As if on cue, my home telephone rang. I looked at the caller id as the words UNKNOWN CALL moved across the display. I didn't want to answer. Actually, I was afraid to answer.

"Hello."

"You are receiving a call from an inmate at Gatesville Correctional Facility. Press one to accept the call, press two to decline."

I wondered who could be calling me from a prison in Texas. I'd never even been to Texas. It was strange. Fear consumed me. I calmed down as I thought about my prayer. I'd asked God to help me. This had to be someone sent to me by The Almighty, to protect me from myself.

I pressed the number one.

"Hello."

"Hello my Kimmee. It's been a long time, how are you?"

The voice on the other line was a woman. Not just any woman though; it was my long lost Aunt Ola. Boy, we hadn't heard from Aunt Ola in years. I'd always wondered where she went. Most of the family thought she was dead; possibly killed by a crazy, deranged John she'd been mixed up with. Alicia and I both knew Aunt Ola was too strong to be murdered by anyone. We knew she was alive. Only we thought she was somewhere hiding. Living high on the hog from a scam she'd come up with. Alicia hated Aunt Ola. I loved her. She'd saved me. My emotions shifted from excitement to worry. Aunt Ola was right on time to save me again. But she was calling from prison. How could this be?

Aunt Ola explained everything to me in one phone call. We talked for two hours. I wasn't sure how she was able to stay connected for such an extended time but she told me that she had a connection in the penitentiary that only money could buy. It was just like Aunt Ola to always find a way to beat the system.

The first thing I wanted to know is how she'd ended up in prison in Gatesville, Texas.

"We've missed you so much Aunt Ola. How did you manage to get yourself in prison?"

"I've missed you girls, too. Think about it, I didn't get the chance to see you all grow into the fine women you are today. You're married to a rich doctor, and my Alicia is a successful business woman. The real estate market is tough, and she's still very accomplished. I'm proud of you all. I wasn't around Kimmee, but I have kept up with your lives."

Aunt Ola paused for a second as if she were holding back tears. I waited for her to go on, but she didn't continue until I prodded her to.

"How long have you been in prison Aunt Ola, and how did you get there?" I asked.

"I killed a man."

Aunt Ola stopped there. I could sense that she was gazing into space. I gave her a moment before prodding further.

"You killed a man? Who? Why?" The frown on my face birthed a headache.

"I killed Alicia's father."

"Alicia's father?" I asked baffled. I didn't realize Alicia's father had been around. None of us knew him.

"Marcus. Marcus was Alicia's father. He didn't know he was her father because I never told him, or Alicia for that matter. The paternity of Alicia's father was never important to me. All I wanted was a little girl of my own, and I used Marcus to have her. Once Alicia was born, I vowed to never tell them because Marcus didn't want children. He was willing and capable of loving another man's child, but he constantly said that he didn't want any of his own. I always left Alicia with Marcus because I never thought he'd hurt her, but that negro fooled me. He touched my baby in ways she should have never been touched and I killed him when you were both little girls. I love Alicia, Kimmee. I would die for her, but instead I was forced to kill for her. I was on the run for years before they caught me. That's why I didn't ever come back. It was to protect Alicia. I knew eventually I'd have to answer for my sins, and I didn't want that to happen while my baby girl was around. Once the police were on to me with solid evidence, I confessed."

My jaw dropped in utter amazement. Finding out that not only had Aunt Ola killed Marcus but that Marcus was Alicia's dad was too much to bear at once. I didn't ask any more questions because I didn't want to hear any more of the truth. I couldn't believe my ears. Aunt Ola spoke again, interrupting as I reflected on the situation.

"I didn't have anything to lose, Kimmee. Nothing at all. My life was over when my baby girl told me that bastard molested her. I've lived all these years as the shell of the woman I used to be. It was easy to take his life; I never gave it a second thought. Love will make you do some strange things, Kimmee. Even commit murder."

There was a long pause after she said those words. I had to change the subject. I didn't want to think about Marcus or what he'd done to my cousin Alicia. So I told Aunt Ola about my relationship with Eddie Lee and how I'd lost my baby. A child I never really wanted, but needed in order to save my marriage. Somewhere along the way, I'd grown to love that little creature, only to lose him. The longer I talked about it, the more distressed I became. This was all Eddie Lee's fault. Aunt Ola agreed. I had to do something about it.

"I love you Aunt Ola. Please don't be a stranger. I can't wait to tell Alicia about your call."

"Don't tell her," Aunt Ola said matter of fact.

"She needs to know Auntie. We've both worried about you for years. She'll be happy to know you're alive and well," I said, trying to convince her.

"Alicia hates me."

"No, she doesn't," I lied.

Aunt Ola knew better. Alicia hated her.

"Respect my wishes. I will work things out with Alicia in due time. All you need to worry about is taking care of that rich husband of yours. So what are you going to do?"

I didn't have an answer for Aunt Ola. I bid her goodbye, but invited her to call me again soon. Then I made a quick decision.

Not long after my suicidal thoughts and talk with Aunt Ola, I went to Monica's house. I sat outside for hours staring at a 3D sonogram photo of my unborn child as I contemplated my next move. There was no way I would let her steal my husband, and celebrate the birth of their child while I mourned the loss of mine. She didn't deserve Eddie Lee or a baby. Finally, I got out the car and walked to the front door and knocked. My husband opened the door.

"What are you doing here? Are you crazy?" he hissed.

"I came to take you home. You're my husband, I love you, and I refuse to let you go so easily."

"How many times do I have to tell you? We're done Kimberlee. I'm not going anywhere. I'm going to stay with Monica and raise our baby."

That's when I put the gun in his face and forced my way inside Monica's home like the intruder I was. He backed up as I walked in; Eddie Lee knew I was serious. He knew I would shoot. I didn't want to hurt my husband, but if I couldn't have him, no one would. I held them hostage for hours. I couldn't believe I was doing it. I didn't want to hurt them. It wasn't worth it, but now that I'd come this far, there was no turning back.

The stress of the situation sent her into labor. Good thing for us, Eddie Lee was a doctor. He delivered the baby without incident, instantly falling in love with her. It was a girl. I started crying, but never put the gun down. I waved it in the air and told them to name her Kimberlee. I told Monica I was taking my husband home with me and we'd raise her baby as ours. She protested like any good mother would. It pissed me off enough to touch the gun to the back of her head and pull the trigger. She died instantly.

No one would keep me from my family.

My husband screamed when I shot her. He had the nerve to be mad because I killed his mistress, and he threatened to call the police on me. I laughed a depraved laugh and told him all of this was his fault. If he'd kept his pants zipped, there would be no issues.

Eddie Lee's reaction infuriated me. I took him out the same way I did her, except I looked him square in the eyes before shooting him in the face. He died holding the baby. I removed her from his arms, and wrapped her in a small blanket. I didn't feel bad at all for what I'd done because this was his fault. Before I left, I took a knife from the kitchen and gutted the bitch. Nobody messed with me and got away with it. I hovered over their bodies for a tad. I couldn't

believe I'd just killed them both. Regret enveloped my entire body.
I stared at the lifeless body of Monica Simmons, wishing I could
undo it all, but I couldn't. Why did I kill her? It wasn't all her fault.
Eddie Lee was to blame. He was a dog chasing cat, and I chose to
kill the cat! I couldn't stand anymore. I had to get out of there!

    It was after four in the morning when I arrived home. Before I
could take a bath and clean the baby, there was a knock on my
front door.

Alicia

The fight with Jared took everything from me. I drove around for a while thinking about my next move. I wasn't sure what to do, but I knew I wasn't going home. The clock on my dashboard said it was four-fifteen, the only place I could think to go at that time of morning was Kimberlee's house. I hadn't seen her in a while, but I was always welcomed there.

I knocked on the door, half expecting her not to answer. I knew it was a weird hour to be knocking, but I didn't want to spend the night in a lonely hotel room. Kimberlee answered the door standing sideways, barefoot and wearing a powder blue terry-cloth robe. She was surprised to see me, but she hadn't been sleep.

"Is everything okay?" she asked, running one hand through her tangled mane.

Something was very wrong. Kimberlee was fidgety, and upon a second look I noticed small red droplets on her housecoat, and a tiny bundle carefully cradled in her arms.

"I'm okay, just need a place to crash for a while, but you look horrible. What's going on with you?"

"I've had a rough night, Alicia. I just -"

A cat-like whimper stopped her mid-sentence. We both looked down. Kimberlee invited me into the house, and finished what she was saying as she walked toward the kitchen.

"Sorry. I'm a mess. I just had the baby."

She said it casually like it was no big deal as she returned from the kitchen with a warm bottle of formula. When she unwrapped the receiving blanket, I noticed more red spots.

"You had the baby! Are you okay? Do you need to see a doctor? Where's Eddie?" I was frantic, and it didn't seem to me that Kimberlee would have been far enough along to give birth, but I saw with my own eyes the baby was here, alive and well.

Kimberlee appeared shaken by the flood of questions. Something serious had happened. The look on her face was frightening. This was weird and it scared me.

"Calm down girl. I'm fine. My husband's a doctor. He delivered the baby here. He's upstairs, and I was about to clean up to go to the hospital, just as a precautionary measure, before you knocked on the door."

She continued to feed the baby. I was still worried. Things were out of whack. We should've been celebrating the birth of her baby together, but Kimberlee hadn't called me to say anything. Even now, she didn't reveal the baby's name, sex, or anything. She asked me to leave before I could find out. Things were getting weirder by the minute. I left because I didn't feel right, and stopped at a hotel a few blocks down to catch some ZZZ's.

I wasn't sleep long before I was awakened by the annoying howling of my cell phone. Of course, it was Jared. He called repeatedly. Finally, I grew tired of the ring, and silenced the phone.

Nightmares took over my sleep like an alien invasion, as sunrays made their way through cracks in the drapery. The room was quiet except for the loud ticking of the clock. I wasn't going to get any sleep so I sat up and turned on the television to drown out the ticking. Breaking news was on every channel. A black woman had been murdered, slaughtered, and gutted like a pig. My stomach turned over. I flipped the TV off. I was already depressed. I didn't need to hear about a gruesome killing.

Tomeka

I woke up butt-naked with a pounding headache and a queasy stomach. My tongue was covered in an icky film; felt hairy like I needed to shave it. I rubbed my head and stomach simultaneously as I blinked a few times. It took me a minute before I remembered what had happened. I wanted it to be a dream. Not in a million years could anyone have told me Malik was screwing Tina. I would've never believed it.

I should have never let Tina so far into my business with Malik. I regretted every detail I'd given her about our past sex life, and I definitely regretted telling her I wasn't giving him none.

I needed to vomit, but the migraine from my hangover wouldn't allow me to move. I lay in bed, just a few minutes longer, until that vile liquid made its way up my esophagus to my mouth. I jumped out of bed, headed for the bathroom. I was in there for fifteen minutes. Everything on my stomach was gone. Now I was dry heaving. I'd had far too much to drink. Alicia tried to stop me, but seeing my man with Tina overtook me. So here I was- a pitiful mess lying on the floor of my bathroom, completely naked, waiting to vomit some more. I don't know how long I lay there, but I must have passed out. I didn't wake until I heard Malik calling my name. I thought I was dreaming because there was absolutely no way he was in the house after last night.

Malik walked into the bathroom, and picked me up from the floor. I didn't want him to touch me, but I was tired of lying there, and I couldn't pull myself together. He led me into the bedroom, where he dressed me in pajamas, before giving me an icepack, some aspirin, saltine crackers, and a Sprite.

"Here baby. Take this. You need to put something on your stomach. The soda should help relieve your nausea."

Baby? He was talking to me like last night didn't happen. An ounce of relief swept over me. Maybe I'd been dreaming.

"Will you answer a question, honestly, Malik?" I didn't want to make assumptions.

"Anything, honey."

"What happened last night?"

Malik was quiet. He averted his eyes to avoid looking at me.

"Malik?"

There was still no answer. I knew I hadn't been dreaming. Malik was at Mary Love's kissing my alleged friend.

"I want you out, Malik!"

He didn't move.

"Now!!!!!" I screamed.

A sudden burst of adrenaline allowed me to move. I threw the icepack at Malik's head, but he didn't flinch.

"What the hell are you waiting for? Get out! Get out! Get out!"

He finally spoke softly, "Are you sure you want me to leave?"

"That's a stupid question, Malik. Get out! I hate you, and I never want to see you again."

"That's not what you said last night."

"Oh really? What did I say last night?" I asked, putting my hands on my hips.

"You said you love me, and you want me to stay. You said we could work it out," he said, still avoiding eye contact with me.

"And when did I say that? I definitely don't remember."

"You said it while we were making love."

"What? Are you saying you stuck that thing in me, and I let you?" I asked hysterically.

Malik reached for me like he wanted to hug me.

"Don't touch me Malik! I was drunk out of my mind. I didn't mean what I said. I saw you kissing my friend in a public place. You humiliated me in front of everyone, then came home and slept with me like it never happened. You took advantage of me, and you disgust me!"

My words didn't faze Malik.

"Meka, baby, listen to me," he said reaching for me again.

"Don't touch me. Do you hear me? I hate you!"

Malik pissed me off each time he reached for me. I needed to get away from him. I shuffled through my purse until I found my cell phone, called my mother, and told her I would be there shortly to get my babies. My head felt like I'd been hit with a sledgehammer, but I was willing to endure the pain to get away from Malik.

"Please listen to me. The kiss with Tina didn't mean anything. I was drunk, she was flirting, and it just happened. I've never looked at her like that before, but she was so aggressive last night. If I'd planned to cheat on you, it wouldn't have been at Mary Love's where you and your friends are always hanging out. We belong together, Tomeka. Last night was a mistake. You deserve the best; that's what I hustle for. I do it all for you and the boys. I wouldn't do it for nobody else."

"Shut up Malik. I don't mean anything to you. All you care about is money, money, money. If you loved me, we wouldn't be here," I said, sobbing uncontrollably.

"Marry me, Meka." He got down in front of me on one knee.

"Get up," I said, turning to walk away.

"Marry me baby," he said following me around on his knees.

"Get up, Malik. You look silly."

"I'm silly for you, Tomeka. I'm sorry about last night. It was the heat of the moment. You turned Christian, and I had to be celibate. We hadn't done it in almost a year. A year, baby. I was weak. What did you want me to do? You have to be fair. You made a vow to God to change your life- I didn't. But I supported your change. I encouraged your change. Do you know how hard it is for a man not to have sex? But I'm still here with you

Tomeka. How is this fair? I put my life on the line everyday so you can live a lavish lifestyle. I'll leave the game, and go to church. Whatever you want, just don't leave me."

As pathetic as it sounds, I felt sorry for Malik. He'd been reduced to begging, and I'd never seen him like this before. The ice around my heart slowly started to melt. He did have a point. How many men would go for me deciding to be celibate? I couldn't name one. Maybe it was unfair of me to expect him to stop having sex, simply because I wanted to change. What if the tables had been turned? What if he'd stopped giving me love and affection?

"Will you be my wife, Tomeka? Will you make our family complete? The only thing missing is a sex life. That's why I've been distant, but we can make this right. I would never ask you to step outside your religion, so let's get married to solve the fornication problem.

"Why now, Malik? What's different today?" I asked seriously.

"I realize I'm about to lose you. I can't go on without you and the boys. Y'all are my world."

"Are you marrying me because of the sex issue?"

"No, baby. I'm marrying you because I love you, and I want to spend the rest of my life with you. I can't lie and say it doesn't have anything to do with making love to you, but that's only a small part. I need you in my life. What do you say? Do you love me? Will you marry me?"

I couldn't answer him immediately. I needed to think it over, and I told him so. I asked him to give me a while to think about it, and he agreed. After our talk, I told him I was going to pick up Khalil and Khalik.

"You don't have to go get them. I had your mom to meet my sister with the twins because she wanted to keep them today. Besides, Meka, we need some alone time. I've turned the ringer off on my cell and the house phone. I'm going to ask you to do the same. Let's spend some quality time together today, just me and you."

Deep down, I wanted to plunge a knife in his heart. I wanted to watch him scream in pain because his heart hurt the same as mine. But there was no denying that I loved Malik and I didn't want to lose him over someone like Tina. I stood there for a moment contemplating if I really wanted to be with him. He asked me again to turn off my cell and spend some quality time with him. The ice on my chest was now a puddle of water. I reached for my cell to turn it off. It rang before I could hit the power button. Malik snatched it, answering before handing it back to me. Alicia was calling to check on me. I told her I was fine. I could hear the disappointment in her voice. She was upset because Malik answered my phone, but I couldn't worry about that. Alicia had her own issues to deal with. She couldn't tell me how to live my life.

Alicia

I sat up on the bed. It was time for me to smoke my breakfast. Inside my purse was the sack of weed from the night before. I didn't have any cigars but I always kept a small pack of joint papers in my coin purse. I licked, tucked, rolled, and then lit the joint. A sense of euphoria calmed my nerves while I replayed the events of the past years in my mind. Things had definitely gone downhill. Two years ago, I loved my life. I loved my friends. I loved the boyfriend who I thought would one day be my husband. I loved the little newborn baby who never escaped my thoughts.

Today, I hate my life. I've lost my friends. I hate my current boyfriend, and the ex-boyfriend, whose mistress I once was. I no longer wanted to be anyone's wife. The only thing that remains the same is my love for the little crumb snatcher who probably won't recognize me when I go to get him back.

I took a long, deep breath, shaking my head, taking another pull from my left hand cigarette. My life was messed up and there was no running from that. I smashed the cherry of my joint in the ashtray, and made my way into the bathroom for my morning pee, careful not to sit on the hotel toilet. I came back out and sat on the edge of the bed. I contemplated lighting my weed back up, but I decided I shouldn't go to work with a buzz. I didn't have any clothes at the hotel with me so I didn't shower there; I had to go home. I hoped Jared was no longer there. I hoped like hell Victoria missed him and he'd gone to comfort her. I officially hated Jared, and if he wasn't going to move out, I was.

On the drive home, I called to check on Tomeka. Malik answered the phone. I hung up in his face. Yeah, I wanted to talk to him about as much as I wanted to talk to Jared. To me, they were no different; two mutts that weren't worthy of good homes. They deserved to live the lives of the strays they were.

My phone rang.

"Hello."

"Did you mean to hang up on me?" It was Malik.

"Oh, no my signal faded. I was calling for Tomeka, is she there?"

"Yeah, hold up."

"It's your homegirl," I heard him say.

I almost hung up again, but sat on hold until she picked up the receiver.

"Hello." She didn't sound too upset.

"Hey girl, what are you doing?"

"Trying to straighten things out with Malik."

"Are you going to stay with him?"

"We have kids, Alicia. I'm not making any promises, but I'm, going to hear him out. I don't want to be a single mother. I'm worthy of better."

"Wow! That didn't take long."

"The Holy Bible teaches us to forgive our transgressors as Jesus forgives us."

"You don't owe me an explanation," I said, almost running a red light.

"We all fall short, Alicia."

"Like I said, you don't owe me an explanation. I was just checking on you. Let me call you back before I kill myself."

"Huh?"

"I almost ran a red light, fooling with you. I'll call you later."

"You mad?"

"Who am I Tomeka? Jesus forgives. Do what makes you happy. Know that I'm here for you. Call me if you need me."

"Love ya."

"Love ya back."

I hung up. I couldn't believe Tomeka was going to take Malik back so soon. It almost pissed me off. But it's her life and if she wants to be miserable who am I to stop her? All I can do is be here for her to help pick up the pieces when Malik shatters her world.

I made it to the office without incident. Jared wasn't home when I went to shower and change, which was the best thing that had happened in a long time.

I was surprised to see Mrs. Young waiting for me when I arrived. I wasn't too happy to see her because she'd asked me to find her another house, and I hadn't even started working on it. My personal life was consuming me. Priority number one was to slow down on drinking alcohol, stop smoking weed, then hire an attorney to help me get custody of Little Omar. Initially, I was trying to work and save the money to retain him, but I didn't have to do that since I'd stolen more than five thousand dollars from Jared before I left Atlanta. I planned to call Jefferson, and have him to put me in contact with his sister who happened to be a family law attorney.

"Well, it's about time you arrived," Mrs. Young said playfully.

"Have you been waiting long? They should have called to tell me you were here." I didn't sound as playful.

"Oh no, baby. I wasn't here long before you got here. I was kidding with you."

"Well, Mrs. Young, what can I do for you today?"

"You can join me at Winky's Seafood for lunch."

I tried to protest, but she wasn't taking no for an answer.

"It's time Alicia. I've been asking you to meet with me and my son for months. I've already set it up. He'll be at Winky's at two o'clock, and so will you and I."

"I'll be there."

I gave in because Mrs. Young had been after me for months. I'd refused the whole time because I was in a relationship with Jared and Mrs. Young was trying to be a matchmaker. She kept telling me how much her son would love me, how much we had in common. Today, she prevailed, but I told her I was fresh out of a relationship, and I wasn't looking for anything new. Mrs. Young assured me the meeting would be nothing like that.

I finished some paperwork, then searched through the MLS for a house that would suit Mrs. Young's needs. I printed some of the matches, deciding I would take them with me to Winky's for her to look over. Mrs. Young called to make sure our lunch date was still on. I grabbed my purse, dug out my car keys, and cell phone, and raced out of the office.

Alicia

Upon entering Winky's I got the surprise of the century. Sitting at the table with Mrs. Young was Mr. Tall, Dark, and Handsome, the man of my nightmares. My stomach did flips. I turned to run out of the restaurant. Mrs. Young caught me before I could escape.

"It's time to face the music, Alicia. You can't run forever."

"You're right. But why did you bring me here to meet him? How do you know Omar?"

"He's my son."

Mrs. Young went on to explain that she didn't always know. She initially wanted us to meet for business reasons, then she saw the picture of Little Omar and put it together. She told Omar she'd found me and gave him my cell number. He'd found out about us hanging at Mary Love's because of Kimberlee's Facebook updates. She updated her status all day, keeping everyone up on the latest. He'd purposely run upon me at Mary Love's.

With Mrs. Young's help, we were able to work things out. We came to a mutual agreement at Winky's. The plan was to start slow. They agreed to let me visit my son at their home every weekend until he was comfortable with me, then I'd be allowed to take him alone. Eventually, I would have custody and they would have visitation.

Mrs. Young's presence in my life had paid off. She was a blessing from God, and I wanted to officially thank Him. When I left Winky's I called Tomeka to tell her I would join her for church on Sunday. I wanted to go to Mary Love's to celebrate, but I decided to stay away for a while.

With things going well for me, I wanted to check on Kimberlee, and share my good news with her. Her cell phone kept going to voicemail. Getting concerned, I called the house.

A policeman answered the phone. They were taking Kimberlee in for murder.

Epilogue

I would love to tell you that things worked out for all of us, but that would be a lie. Jared and I tried to repair our relationship, but too much damage had been done. He'd succeeded at being an Omar impersonator and I hated him. I learned a valuable lesson: I was looking for love in all the wrong places. For now, I will focus on establishing a bond with my son, and when the time comes for love, I'll put the batteries in my plastic, vibrating boyfriend.

Kimberlee's story ended the day she killed her husband and his mistress. Technically though, it didn't end until it had been narrated on that crazy show, *Snapped*. In the end, she had no remorse. She was driven to the brink, crossing that thin line between love and hate. Love drove her to hate, hate drove her to kill. Hate prevailed and all hope was gone for her. Now she will live the rest of her life, confined like a caged animal. As for the baby, she was put into the foster care system for a short time before Kimberlee's mom adopted her. In some sick way, she felt like the baby would replace Kimberlee's presence in her life.

Tomeka and Malik were married on the snow-white sands of Nassau, Bahamas. They recently celebrated their one-year anniversary. Don't get it wrong, by no means was it a fairytale ending for the two of them. They have ups and downs but, they're handling things. Malik started going to church with Tomeka and kept his promise to get out the game, but not before he used some of his earnings to pay college tuition. He is back in school, studying to be an athletic trainer. It's not a job that will give them a lavish lifestyle, unless of course he gets a job with the NFL, but starting off, it will be enough to help. Besides, while Malik was gambling his life in the streets, Tomeka made some major moves. She invested enough of the drug money to live good for a while. Yeah, they call that money laundering but my girl did whatever it would take to be okay. Don't worry about the two of them, they're straight.

After it all, Omar and his wife were hard to deal with. As it turns out, the offer they'd made at Winky's was to please Mrs. Young. Not long after the promise, we were in court fighting for custody. They won the battle, but I was given visitation and ordered to pay child support which was a hard pill to swallow, but it served me right. I'd failed at punishing Omar. What I did was wrong, and God don't like ugly, so it backfired on me. Just like My Dear's stay in Gatesville prison serves her. The good news for me is that my son will know me. I will never miss a visit or a payment. I will work on my relationship with him, and maybe one day I'll stop beating myself up over it. One thing's for sure, I won't end up like My Dear, which is what I fought so hard for all these years.

We all fought our own battles with our hearts and we've all learned from them. Just so happens that for some of us, it was too late.

Shekia Mason was born and raised in the small town of Jasper, Texas. She discovered her love of writing when she was forced to deal with the tragic shooting of her younger brother. She penned her first work, Make Me Stronger back in 2009. In 2011, she wrote and self-published Anyone Wanna Buy a Heart, which was originally released as A Bruised Heart. With the success of that novel, she signed a deal and penned Anyone Wanna Buy a Heart 2 and The Black Sheep under Kiki Swinson. She is currently co-writing a book titled Flawed and All with Nikki Rountree and has recently started a media company, Two Queens Media with her partner Ashley Cruse.

Facebook: https://www.facebook.com/shekia.mason

Instagram & Twitter: @gensanity

ABOUT THE AUTHOR FROM ALL HER FRIENDS...

SHEKIA IS...

A very beautiful, vivacious, strong-minded and determined young lady who I'm very proud of. --

Arenthia Spikes (Mama)

Brilliant and has and will continue to inspire the lives of others. – **Toya Crisp**

My inspiration, my sister, auntie to my daughters, and my best friend. –**Tomekia Oliver (Winky)**

The friend who I would want as a sister if I had one, she is an inspiration in my life, she is the friend I need to just tell me things that I really do not want to hear, but need to hear.-- **Tyesha "Ty" Mustin**

The only person in this world that I can go to for ABSOLUTELY anything. –**Raynell**

Beautiful, strong and independent. –**Shea Norwood**

My sister, my friend and confidant, and my trigger to success! – **Nieka Spikes**

Best described by her lofty accomplishments and even higher expectations of success. –**Ed Provitt, Jr.**

Energetic, passionate, and determined. –**Jamal Douglas**

A strong, black woman who is beautiful, kind, and classy – **Richard Prince**

An independent woman who is a self-motivated overachiever that doesn't only shoot for the sky but the stars instead. –Xavier Spikes

www.ingramcontent.com/pod-product-compliance
Lightning Source LLC
Chambersburg PA
CBHW020728210626
46807CB00016B/483

9 780692 677988